Death of a Big Man

This story is told by Charles Ripley, once a Chief Superintendent of police, now a retired cripple having been shot in the
back in the course of duty.

Among all the villains Ripley met one stands out in his
memory: Paul Gunter, utterly callous and ruthless, courageous
to the point of indifference to any risk. He has become a lead-
ing gangster, head of protection rackets, with power and
antennae throughout the northern city. Ripley hates him—and
hates him even more after he has deliberately goaded a room full
of policemen at the retirement party given by Chief Superintendent Collins.

One or two senior policemen find their anger has outrun the
restraints of duty and the law. A cabal is formed with intent to
murder Gunter privately.

There are many threads to this complex and thrilling book. One
is a study of incapacity, the detailed pain and frustration of a
crippled man.

Perhaps this is John Wainwright's very best book—praise
indeed. The story develops with marvellous subtlety, the end is
shocking and astounding—but it can be seen to be true.

By the same author

DEATH IN A SLEEPING CITY
TEN STEPS TO THE GALLOWS
EVIL INTENT
THE CRYSTALLISED CARBON PIG
TALENT FOR MURDER
THE WORMS MUST WAIT
WEB OF SILENCE
EDGE OF EXTINCTION
THE DARKENING GLASS
THE TAKE-OVER MEN
THE BIG TICKLE
PRYNTER'S DEVIL
FREEZE THY BLOOD LESS COLDLY
THE LAST BUCCANEER
DIG THE GRAVE AND LET HIM LIE
NIGHT IS A TIME TO DIE
REQUIEM FOR A LOSER
A PRIDE OF PIGS
HIGH-CLASS KILL
THE DEVIL YOU DON'T
A TOUCH OF MALICE
THE EVIDENCE I SHALL GIVE
CAUSE FOR A KILLING
KILL THE GIRLS AND MAKE THEM CRY
THE HARD HIT
SQUARE DANCE

DEATH OF
A
BIG MAN

JOHN WAINWRIGHT

M

SBN: 333 17960 9 ✓

First published 1975 by
MACMILLAN LONDON LIMITED
London and Basingstoke
Associated companies in New York
Dublin Melbourne Johannesburg and Delhi

Printed in Great Britain by
NORTHUMBERLAND PRESS LIMITED
Gateshead

This one is for Avis ... and we both know why!

We all labour against our own cure;
    for death is the cure of all diseases.

Religio Medici
Sir Thomas Brown
1605-1682

The name is Ripley—Charles Ripley—and I'm a copper ... and if that sounds like the opening to an American cops-and-robbers soap opera, that is too bad, and your taste in T.V. entertainment does not rate very high.

And, already, I have told a lie.

I, who had intended to tell this thing without flippery. Without fancy nuances. Without giving a damn about who I hurt, or who I did not hurt—and that including myself—have started all wrong. I have started with an untruth.

I am not a copper ... I am an *ex*-copper.

And even that is only a half-truth because (as if you didn't know!) once a copper, always a copper. Come retirement—come resignation—and you merely hand in the warrant card, the staff and the handcuffs. You merely hang up the uniform, and spend your nights in bed. It is not an ending, or a re-birth. It is not even a new way of life—not really—because policing has also to do with the way you think, and no man can direct his thoughts along certain lines for a quarter of a century and then, on a given day, think differently.

Nevertheless, and strictly by the book, I am an *ex*-copper.

I reached rank. I ended up chief superintendent in a county constabulary; the Law-enforcement Godfather of a four-hundred-square-mile bailiwick of open countryside and market towns—of villages and isolated hilltop farmsteads—called Beechwood Brook. I like to think I was a good copper—a good divisional officer— a general (if you like) with a small army of around three hundred

9

troops (coppers, C.I.D. and clerks) who fought guerilla war against villains who had ambitions of becoming big men ... and some of whom *would* have become big men, had we not stopped them in time. I like to think we (myself, and the men and women who obeyed my orders) did a real 'preventive' job; that we shattered the hopes of some bastards with big ideas and, in so doing, eased the future burden of the city and the met. boys ... some city, or the capital, always being the Mecca of which these bastards dream.

That is what I like to think.

But (as always) and however hard we tried, some slipped the net. Some got through ... Gunter got through.

So-o—if this thing has a logical starting place—maybe I should start with Gunter.

Paul Gunter.

The first time I saw him, I knew he was different. Unique, and potential dynamite. He didn't scare ... and, by that, I mean *just* that. It wasn't an act; it wasn't the usual four-by-two, up-you-pig routine every copper expects when he walks into an interview room and faces the man he has to break. Gunter just was *not* scared.

He even nodded a brief greeting. Not friendly, but full of meaning. It said, 'Start talking, copper—start slugging, if that's the sort you are ... see if I care.'

And (damn him to hell!) he *didn't* care.

He was inside for using a hammer on some young village tease who'd led him on, then crossed her legs at the last minute. Some will argue that she deserved all she got—but they didn't see her ... she didn't deserve what *she* got. Her face will remain ugly and broken, for the rest of her life, and only the Angel of God stopped the jagged edge of a broken rib from puncturing something vital and making her bleed to death, from inside.

That was the size of the beat-up ... and he didn't give a damn.

He just sat there—thick, black-haired arms resting easily on the interview-room table—knowing we had enough eye-witnesses, and evidence to send him to hell ... and he didn't give a damn about that, either.

Like every other copper with a small lifetime of bobbying behind him, I could interview. I could question, I could lean, I could hit a suspect with enough words to make him dizzy—to make him ready to drop his own grandmother ... but not this one.

He sat there. Not smiling, not looking cocky, not looking anything (except, maybe, slightly bored) and, here and there, saying, 'Okay. Prove it.' Not saying one word to help himself, because that same word might also help us; knowing we *could* prove it—knowing we *would* prove it ... but still not giving a damn.

I left that interview room more rattled than Gunter was; I left it feeling like a heavyweight champ who has just been toppled from his throne by some unknown brawler. Coppers shouldn't feel that way. It was bad for their ego. Nine-hundred-and-ninety-nine times from every thousand they *don't* feel that way ... but this was my thousandth time.

I'd met Paul Gunter.

Okay—we proved the G.B.H. and Gunter earned himself five years ... and even that might have only been three, had he shown an ounce of respect for the man wearing the wig and ermine. Judges, like cops, are human but judges, unlike cops, can bite back. But (I'll tell you something) I watched Gunter's face as he left the dock and—I swear!—the teeth hadn't even punctured the skin.

That was Gunter. The only time I ever handled him. Before I became chief superintendent; when I was a raw 'super', new to Beechwood Brook, and before Beechwood Brook Division swallowed up Pike Top Division in an amalgamation shake-up and made the patch big enough to warrant a chief superintendentship.

Before I knew Henry Collins. Before I knew David Raff. Before I knew Dick Sullivan.

As long ago as that.

And yet ...

Gunter haunted me. No—that's wrong ... the *memory* of Gunter haunted me. The size of the man; the size of the man's personality; the size of the man's self-confidence. Measured in any direction, and by any yardstick, Gunter was a giant. It wasn't that he broke the law. It wasn't as simple as that. He *made* the law—his own law ... then he enforced it. The other stuff—the ordinary law, which ordinary men obeyed, or were punished for disobeying—was a minor nuisance. A trivia. Something he learned to brush aside via the terror of his own displeasure, or the use of a well-paid lawyer.

To the best of my knowledge, that five-year sentence was the only one Paul Gunter ever heard a judge pronounce. He disappeared behind prison walls and, when he returned to decent society, he did not return to Beechwood Brook. He made for the city and became, first, the problem of Raff and then, the problem of Sullivan. He licked them both ... and the man who can lick Dick Sullivan is the sort of man around whom strato-cruisers must make a detour!

I watched it all, from the side-line, and thanked God it was them, and not me.

I watched Gunter. I watched how he operated. I watched what he did ... watched but, like Raff and Sullivan, could do damn-all about it.

Gunter did not waste time scrambling to the top of any ready-made dung heap. He kicked all the other dung heaps to hell, then built his own. Mountain-high and firmly based upon a triple-foundation of graft, fear and corruption. He ran all the rackets in the city; protection, skin-flicks, clip-joints, disco-halls, bordelloes ... the lot! What he didn't run, personally, he was behind. And the handful of legitimate, hole-in-the-wall dumps geared to shake loose change from the pockets of the mugs did so only with his consent ... a consent which had to be paid for.

And the more powerful he became, the more powerful he was able to become. It works that way. The first stop is to get big ... getting bigger just happens, naturally.

He spread his operations. He took in other cities—other towns —other territories, until he was the biggest thing outside the

M.P.D. ... and second only to a couple of *their* 'firms'.

And we, the cops (the *honest* cops) writhed in anguish, because we couldn't halt him. We knew, but we couldn't prove. Raff damn near drove himself crazy. Sullivan squirted blue smoke from every aperture in his body. Even Collins lost his eternal 'cool'.

For what good it did!

Then Gunter committed the ultimate sin ... he killed a policeman.

A nothing—a nobody—a detective constable with visions of reaching the top in one giant stride ... by nailing the great Paul Gunter. And all the poor bastard did was make a nuisance of himself. Nothing more than that. He could have been cleared, beyond the horizon, with one dropped hint.

But Gunter was Gunter, and Gunter had his own way of dealing with nuisances; a way which was final and, and the same time, a warning to all other potential nuisances.

The grapevine said that Gunter himself squeezed the trigger, prior to his heavies dumping the body of the dead D.C. into the stinking waters of the canal basin. The grapevine said it, because Gunter decreed that the grapevine say it ... and, moreover, that it be believed without qualification. It was his own unique 'Trespassers Will Be Prosecuted' notice.

So ...?

Gunter was entertaining two aldermen and a magistrate, at the time of the murder, so Gunter wasn't even interviewed. Because no copper on God's earth can crack an alibi of that class ... not if it's backed by what Gunter reputedly had on the trio of bastards who shielded him from common justice.

Paul Gunter ... the man who killed a cop, and got away with it.

And me—Charles Ripley—the only copper who ever put him down.

I think this thing started in that interview room, long time gone, when I recognised Gunter for what he was. That rarest of all animals, the true rogue male of the human species.

*　　*　　*

So, let us say that this thing started, all those years back, in an interview room at Beechwood Brook nick.

Then, let us say I'm wrong ...

Come forward a decade, or so, and there is another 'starting point'.

Still in Beechwood Brook area but, this time, up there on the tops; and a trigger-happy lunatic was pushing off shots all ways and everywhere; when one of those shots nicked my spine and, in a shared second of eternity turned me from 'copper' to '*ex*-copper'.* Nobody's fault—not really ... the man was temporarily out of his mind and (anyway) he wasn't aiming at anybody or anything. I just happened to be in the way and, because I just happened to be in the way, I don't know what is going on south of my waist, my legs are in irons and I walk (walk!) only with the aid of elbow crutches.

Does that have overtones of bitterness?

If so, I make no apology. I try not to be bitter—correction ... I try not to *show* my bitterness. But this (above all else) has to be honest—it has to be a complete stripping of the soul, otherwise it is nothing—and at night, when I am alone in my bed, the bitterness takes over and damn near chokes me and, if I were a weeping man, I would weep.

Why me? Why had it to be *me*?

Come to that, why had it to be *anybody*?

One sufficient answer—one answer I could accept—to that question (to both these questions) and the bitterness would sweeten and I would, perhaps, revert to the man I think I once was.

But that answer does not exist, therefore ...

Therefore it can equally well be argued that this thing started on the Wendell Moor tops, with a wildly fired bullet and a certain Chief Superintendent Charles Ripley who happened to be an inch (no more than two inches) too far to the right.

That, too, could be a 'starting point'.

*　　　*　　　*

* *A Touch of Malice,* by John Wainwright—Published by Macmillan 1973.

14

As, also, could be the death of my wife ... in which case, the 'starting point' is only a mere two years ago. Slightly less than two years—one year, nine months and four days ... to be precise. I could pinpoint it in hours—in minutes, and almost in seconds ... and every second a lonely lifetime.

Elaine ...

I will not bore you with a love story. Just that she was a copper's wife—*my* wife—and that she left me, once ... not because I was ever in love with another woman, but because I was too much in love with my job. I re-courted her, won her back and, thereafter, knew her true worth.

When the bullet hit me—when the medics were through with me—they swore I was wheelchair-bound for the rest of my life; a cripple, who would never again stand upright.

Elaine called them liars. Not to their faces, but to me; she was my guts and my determination, my bloody-mindedness and my last hope. She said I would walk again ... and she was right.

I walk—albeit with leg-irons and elbow crutches—I nevertheless walk ... because Elaine said I would.

Maybe it killed her. I'll never know. Externally, she fought my battle while, internally, she fought her own; to be the wife of such a man and to take, and understand, his savagery—his moods of boiling rage—at what had happened ... and never, ever, to show irritation, or anger, or even undue sympathy. That was her own private battle, secretly fought and without complaint.

She won them both—her own battle, and mine ... and I think it killed her.

Heart attacks give no warning. They just happen and, if they are bad enough, they kill instantly.

Hers was bad enough.

And there was a moment—the blackest, the sourest, the most bitter moment of my whole life—when the curtains were drawn aside, and the coffin slid through the hatch and into the darkness, and I had to stand and watch. To stand and watch, on leg-irons and elbow crutches; pinned there; held, helpless in the iron-mongery she'd worked so hard for me to use; unable to throw myself onto the moving coffin—through the hatch—and embrace her in the flames ... where I, too, belonged.

Somebody—some damn, sanctimonious-tongued idiot—described her death as sudden and like the blowing out of a candle. But not me ... to me, it was like a turning off of the sun. One year, nine months and four days, ago.

And that, also can be taken as a 'starting point'.

But (and I make this admission freely, and without qualification) all these things—my first meeting with Paul Gunter, my crippling and my bereavement—are very *personal* moments, and perhaps not 'starting points' at all ... not the start of the real story. If not then, at least, they are moments of preparation and, without them, what happened could never have happened.

Equate them, then, to the tuning up of the various sections of some great orchestra, prior to the opening bars of a Wagnerian overture.

Equate them with that ... and I'll be satisfied.

But if *they* were the gathering of instruments upon the note A, the down beat came at Collins's retirement party.

God and all His angels know why I went to that damn party ... I don't! I'd been invited—of course I'd been invited—personally, and almost pleadingly, by Collins himself. We were more than fellow-coppers, and fellow-rankers ... we were friends. We had (to use the terminology) sorted some out, together. Some good 'uns. Including a few murder enquiries. He in the city force, me in the adjoining county force, as fellow superintendents and (later) fellow chief superintendents. Both uniform coppers and both (and equally arrogantly) occasionally bopping the C.I.D. crowd in the eye and showing them how crime *should* be detected.

We were both of an age—my own retirement party would have been within weeks of Collins's—but not of a type ... and maybe the difference created the bond and, over the years, strengthened it.

Collins was (to use Elaine's words) 'one of nature's perfect gentlemen'.

16

He was, too. In all the years I knew him I can count the number of times he lost his temper on the fingers of one hand ... and keep the thumb as a non-starter for the number of times I heard him swear. He didn't need to blow his stack, any more than he needed to use strong language to get his message across. He was an educated man. He could use the Queen's English like D'Artagnan could use a sword and, if you were at the receiving end of one of Collins's quietly spoken rockets, you could feel the sparks burning all the way down from your arse to the soles of your socks.

He had what is these days known as charisma—what we, of my generation, used to call character—and, because of this, his men loved him ... and (please note) I use the word 'loved' and not 'liked' because, whereas many men are liked, very few men are *loved*. Especially coppers ... and by coppers.

The Collinses of this world are a moon's march apart, but I knew one of them and could call him 'friend' ... which, I suppose, is one reason why I went to his retiring party.

They were all there. Dick Sullivan—Assistant Chief Constable (Crime) to Collins's own force. David Raff—now retired, as a result of a mental breakdown—now recovered (or *almost* recovered, except for the little-boy-lost look which always peeps out from the back of the eyes) ... one-time detective chief superintendent and the city force's Head of C.I.D. Child ... the present Head of C.I.D. Sweetapple—*Amadeus* Sweetapple, for Christ's sake! (what a combination name to be lumbered with!) ... present gaffer of North End Division; the slum of the city, and the division Sullivan had fisted into daily submission prior to moving up the promotion rungs to his present rank.

Those were the top brass—some of them ... grass roots bobbying was also well represented. It wouldn't have been Collins's 'do' otherwise. Uniform. C.I.D. Motor Patrol. Admin. Clerks. Sergeants and constables. They were all there—forty, maybe fifty ... and their wives.

And rank was forgotten. It didn't even exist.

The main room of *The Woodchopper's Arms* was crowded with coppers, and their womenfolk, as I entered, spotted an empty seat in a comparatively quiet corner and eased and fumbled my way towards it.

I passed within hearing distance of Sullivan. He was having hell's own argument with a not-so-old Motor Patrol constable about the merits and demerits of Yorkshire cricket.

Sullivan was saying, 'Take Boycott. He's the ...'

'Jesus, not *Boycott*!' The constable spoke as from a broken and disappointed heart.

'The finest batsman ever to carry a bat to a crease,' insisted Sullivan.

'A bloody computer,' wailed the constable. 'Every time he straps on his pads he's figuring out his possible average.'

'A machine—agreed ... a run-scoring machine.'

'Without heart. Without *enjoyment*.'

Sullivan glared a little, and said, 'Runs, for Christ's sake. That's what the game's about. Runs.'

'And enjoyment.'

'All right. Enjoyment. Boycott enjoys playing cricket.'

'Look—I mean from the spectator's point of view. He doesn't give *them* enjoyment.'

'*I* like watching him,' said Sullivan, doggedly.

The constable said, 'You're bloody soon pleased,' drained his glass and added, 'My go ... what are you having?'

'Bitter.' Sullivan tipped what was left in his own glass down his throat, and handed the glass to the constable. As the constable turned, Sullivan said, 'I'll be back by the time you've pushed your way to the bar. I'm for a leak.'

Like I say—no rank—it wasn't merely forgotten, it didn't even exist ... not at Collins's 'do'.

I reached the seat I'd been aiming for, lowered myself into a sitting position and leaned the elbow crutches against the wall. I craned my neck in search of a waiter, couldn't see one but, instead, noticed my next-door drinking neighbour.

David Raff ... and, beyond David, Gwen Raff, his wife.

He smiled—a gentle, timid smile—and said, 'Charlie.'

'David.' I nodded my friendship back to him, and said, 'How's life?'

'Being lived. Y'know ... being lived.'

Gwen Raff leaned across, and said, 'A drink, Mr Ripley? Shall I go get you ...'

'No! There'll be a waiter.'

My interruption of the offer was brusque—at least that ... almost rude. It was uncalled for, but it was answered by a kindly and quirky half-smile which held complete understanding, and no rebuke.

I'd never met Gwen Raff before, but a thought struck me ... that she and Elaine should have swapped notes. They both understood the moods and the manners of men who have to live with the worm of self-pity gnawing away at their guts. They'd both learned how to tolerate such a man ... and the not-so-easy way.

I felt a bastard. I wanted to apologise ... but I didn't know how.

I looked around for a waiter, and saw Collins for the first time.

He threaded his way across the room and placed a double whisky, mixed with its own weight in iced water, on the table in front of me.

He said, 'I'm delighted you could come, Charles.'

I muttered something about it being time I went out on a booze-up, and fumbled in my pockets for money.

'No.' Collins waved a hand. 'Everybody's first drink is on me. After all, it's *my*—er—"coming out" party.' He chuckled, quietly, at this non-jokey joke, then continued, 'I've told Harry, the landlord. He'll keep his eyes on you. When you require a re-fill, just glance ... he'll come across. Now—if you'll excuse me for a while—I think I'm expected to—er—*circulate*.'

It was pure 'Collins'. I could never imitate it ... tell it as it really happened. Gentlemanly—but without being smooth ... 'one of nature's perfect gentlemen'. What he'd said (no—the way he'd said it) stopped me feeling an interloper. I was back with them, again—back within the warm circle of the most select club in the whole world ... the British Police Service. I was still a member. An honorary member, perhaps ... but still a member. Sponsored, seconded and voted in unanimously, by Henry Collins.

19

I took a deep swig of the whisky and water and, contrary to what I'd expected, began to enjoy myself a little.

There was talk; a sea of talk into which flowed each group's river of conversation. And, like every other sea, the sea of talk had tides; they rose and fell, then rose to fall again. The waves rolled from end to end of that room in *The Woodchopper's Arms,* then back again and, now and again, one of the waves broke to send a spray of words and memories over nearby groups. Clean memories—purged pure by the passage of time—but always with the sad, salt-taste of 'never again'.

('The time old Harper found that sack, thrown in a hedge-bottom.'

'Y'mean the dead piglet?'

'Aye—remember?—he didn't open the sack. Just felt it ... thought it was a dead baby.'

'Who wouldn't? Y'know ... who *wouldn't*?'

'Sure. But a Murder Alert, for a dead piglet. The whole shooting match—before they got round to opening the sack ... *for a dead piglet.*'

'Poor old Harper. He never lived it down.'

'Where is he, these days?'

'Milk Marketing Board ... last I heard. He retired, moved house, then landed a job with ...')

A sea of talk. Bobby talk. Eddies of conversation; but not in tightly grouped cliques, because the eddies swelled and expanded to include other eddies, then broke up again to become different eddies. Whirlpools of relaxed memory created by men (and women) with memories worthy of remembrance. Good men—and good women—some a little raucous, some already a little worse for drink ... but, to a man, and to a woman, *good* men and *good* women.

('... the night Williamson arrested the super? Gawd strewth! You should have been in the station that night ... when he brought him in.'

'Williamson made a mistake. He was a good copper—still is ... he just made a mistake.'

'Yes—I know—but ...'

'He thought he'd nicked the car. That's all. Williamson didn't know him—he was new to the division ... and, anyway, Purvey was in civvies.'

'I know—but ...'

'Look—you come across some berk in a motor car. Making a complete balls up of starting the thing ...'

'It was a new car. Purvey'd only got it that morning.'

'You ask him for the registration number, and he can't tell you.'

'As I say, he'd only got it ...'

'And he's damn-all identification to say who he is.'

'He *told* Williamson he was Superintendent Purvey.'

'Big deal! Purvey doesn't even look like a copper. He suffers too much from duck's disease.'

'Still ...'

'Williamson did the right thing. The chief said so.'

'Still ...'

'Where is Williamson, now?'

'He moved. Some Midland force. Wise ... after *that* Purvey was gunning for him.'

'Purvey always was a no-good prick ...')

Likes and dislikes. But never hatreds. Even with a man like Purvey (a man I didn't know, and had never met—but I'd met enough of his kind) it was only dislike, tinged with scorn. The scorn of the complete policeman for the copper who is just-short-of-the-complete-policeman. But no hatred.

A thought struck me ... that coppers never *hate* coppers. Except, of course, bent coppers ... and, sure as hell, they hate *them*! But not stupid coppers—not incompetent coppers—not thick-headed coppers. These they tolerate and, often, excuse. Sometimes (as with the unknown Purvey) the toleration and the excusing is stretched too far, and it becomes dislike ... but never hatred.

Meanwhile, I was into my second double whisky and water and was feeling more relaxed. Collins had called at the table a couple of times, stopped for a brief chat, then moved on to perform his duty as host. Sullivan had wandered across, asked about the legs, accepted a non-committal answer and changed the subject, chewed over old times for about fifteen minutes, then left to elbow his way back to the bar.

At one end of the bar two men argued with each other. Coppers —I guessed they were coppers ... although one looked anything *but* a copper. Imagine a gasometer arguing with an oak tree ... that was the impression. The 'gasometer' was fat enough to earn the description 'obese'; his gut stuck out like an eight-month-gone woman carrying quads; he was bald, except for whisps of greying hair above the ears, and his dress was loud enough to drown a pop group ... wide check, with a predominance of reds and greens. His companion topped him by at least four inches; heavy built and white maned; broad shouldered and with that perpetual near angry arrogance which spelled 'top cop' in any language.

I didn't know them.

I asked Raff, and he told me. The fat man's name was Lennox. His companion's name was Sugden. Top jacks from a nearby city force ... men Collins had had dealings with and whom he'd come to like.

It was good enough for me. Whatever they looked, they were good men ... they were friends of Henry Collins.

It was I who was the fool. It was I who broached the forbidden subject.

We were a group—Raff, his wife and a woman sitting beyond Gwen Raff who, or so it seemed, had come with the Raffs—and, although other coppers and their womenfolk strolled over, joined us for a while, then left, we four stayed together; a quartet—two men, two women—who were with all the others but, in some strange way, slightly apart.

Put it down to the booze, if you must have a reason ... I was a hundred miles from being drunk but, if you must have a reason, put it down to the booze. Myself? ... for what it's worth, I like to think I was more relaxed than I'd been for years; that, in this sea of talk, I'd found a haven in which (albeit only for a little time) I could anchor up and forget the gales of emotion which raged outside the walls of *The Woodchopper's Arms*.

I asked a question. It was a question born of genuine concern and honest friendship and, that it was asked with a smile, made it no less concerned and no less friendly.

I asked it of Gwen Raff.

I moved my head in a gesture at Raff, and said, 'How is he, these days?'

She blinked—almost jerked her whole body at the unexpectedness of the question—then visibly sought a hurried answer.

'Mad.' Raff's reply to my damn-fool question was soft-spoken and sour. 'Mad as a bloody hatter ... but I've learned to hide it more than I could.'

'David!' pleaded his wife.

The woman sitting beyond Gwen Raff murmured, 'Take it easy, David. I'm sure Mr Ripley didn't mean to imply ...'

'Oh, I'm *sure*,' muttered Raff.

'He's better—much better.' Gwen Raff answered my question. 'He's almost cured.'

Raff's mouth curled contemptuously.

I muttered, 'Sorry ... I'm sorry, David.'

And I *was* sorry. God help me ... no man could have been sorrier. But, having dropped the brick, I didn't know how to pick it up again. I'm useless at apologising; I haven't the ability; I want to—I truly *want* to—but it always comes out wrong. It always makes things worse.

I wished Collins was around. He'd have known what to say.

Or Elaine. Elaine would have known. Elaine wouldn't have let me drop the brick, in the first place; she'd have guided the conversation; like Collins, she'd have made everything simple—easy—without prickles and without awkward pauses. She'd have ...

'We're cripples, Charlie.' Raff's tone was smeared thick with self-pity. 'You, and me ... and Paulette, there.' He nodded his head towards the woman sitting beyond his wife. 'You're physically crippled. I'm mentally crippled. She's—she's ... *maritally* crippled. The "Cripples Corner" this mate. Everybody pops across to say "Hello" … to do their duty, as decent Christians. Mustn't get drunk—mustn't get too pissed—before we toddle across and let the cripples know we've noticed 'em … occasionally. That we haven't forgotten them … *yet*.'

'Cut it out, David,' I growled. 'We haven't …'

'Oh, you're all right, Charlie. You're all right.' The self-pity had something else in it, now. Something rotten. Something even worse—far worse—than self-pity. He said, 'What happened to you makes you a bloody hero … but not *me*. You stopped a bullet. You deserve a medal. Paulette—her husband, too … *he* deserved a medal. But not me! I just cracked up. I just couldn't take the pressure … so I went round the corner.'

'*You're not mad*.' Gwen Raff ground the words out in a harsh whisper; as if she'd spoken them thousands, and tens of thousands, of times already; as if they were some rote which Raff had to learn, but which he doggedly refused to learn. She said, 'Damn it, David—you had a nervous breakdown … that's all. The work —the strain … it can happen. It *does* happen. You're almost out of it—almost out of the tunnel … for heaven's sake, stop pitying yourself and you'll be *there*.'

'Pity!' Raff made the word a tool of utter contempt. 'That's all they have left to give us. That's why they come across, and talk … then leave. To show their compassion. Their stinking pity. Collins—when he …'

'Collins is a good man,' I cut in. 'Collins invited us—you, me, all of us—because he likes us, not because …'

'Pity!' spat Raff, contemptuously.

I made my voice into a soft snarl, and said, 'David—I heard it on the television—but it's worth repeating. It says so much … especially to people like you, and people like me. "Sympathy"— you'll find it in the dictionary, where it belongs … between "shit" and "syphilis".'

The woman he'd called Paulette breathed, 'Oh, my God!' and, for a moment, I thought the language had shocked her.

Then I looked at her face. It was paper-white and wide-eyed and she was gripping the knuckle of a forefinger between her teeth.

24

I turned my head to see what she was staring at ... and saw Paul Gunter.

And, suddenly, the sea vanished—the waves quietened—and, instead of a sea there was a millpond, scummed over with enmity and alive with the larvae of violence.

The coppers eased their womenfolk into the background; guided them towards the walls and alcoves of the room, and out of harm's way. The coppers who were seated unfolded themselves from their stools and chairs. Those with drinks in their hands, placed their glasses on the nearest tables. There was a gentle movement—like tall grass caught in the first breath of a hurricane—then a freezing of the movement as Sullivan murmured, 'Quieten it down, boys.'

Gunter smiled. The three heavies who were with him grinned, openly, at this moral victory. A photographer—a young, bearded type, from the local press—held his camera at the ready ... even *he* knew something was going to explode. Something! Something the big dailies would give their eyes for.

Gunter strolled to the bar. Unhurriedly. Utterly confident.

He said, 'One whisky, please ... and a chaser.'

'Don't serve him,' said Sullivan, quietly.

'He'd *better*.' Once more, Gunter smiled. 'Read up on your law, Sullivan. This is an "inn". I'm a "traveller". It's not an unreasonable time. It's not an unreasonable request ... and I'm stone-cold sober. He'd *better* serve me. That, or whistle goodbye to his licence at the next Brewster Sessions.'

Harry, the landlord, looked miserable. He asked Sullivan a question, with his eyes.

Sullivan moved his head in a single nod, then said, 'Go ahead ... serve him.'

The grins on the faces of the heavies widened.

Something had to blow. Every man in that room knew it ... every man, and every woman. Each second of silence carried a thousand volts, and the voltage was piling up, and the discipline which Sullivan wielded was a transformer, and the transformer could only hold so much before it burned out.

25

Something *had* to blow.

Harry, the landlord, fumbled with the glasses. He measured the whisky and placed the glass on the bar counter, and the surface of the whisky moved as it took up the tremble of Harry's fingers.

Sullivan gave orders with his eyes—with tiny movements of his head—silent orders which were, in turn, obeyed in silence and without question. A half-circle of space was formed around Gunter; a three-deep arc of cold-eyed coppers which stretched from bar counter to bar counter; every man standing shoulder-to-shoulder and jostling Gunter's trio of heavies until a wall of muscle separated them from their master ... and the heavies exchanged worried scowls for their previous grins.

And something had to *blow*!

Harry pulled a half-pint of mild and placed it, alongside the whisky, on the bar counter. Gunter moved his head in a gentle, unhurried gesture of thanks, felt in his pocket, pulled out a handful of change and began to count coins onto the bar counter top. He ignored the curved phalanx of coppers who hemmed him in. In his own way—with his own arrogant magic—he did more than merely ignore them ... as far as he was concerned, they weren't even there.

But something had to blow!

Gunter picked up the whisky. He turned—deliberately and unhurriedly—and rested the small of his back against the edge of the bar counter. He looked beyond the coppers—above their heads and (or so it seemed) through them. He looked at the table at which we were seated—Raff, Gwen Raff, the woman called Paulette and myself—he raised an eyebrow a fraction, smiled, lifted the glass as if in a toast, and spoke.

Everybody in the room heard the words.

'Your very good health ... Mrs Fixby.'

There was a tiny, ripping sound. The woman called Paulette had been holding a lace-edged handkerchief and, as Gunter spoke, her fingers clenched round its fragile material; her muscles jerked and the handkerchief was shredded. She looked as if she might faint, and never—*ever*—have I seen such concentrated loathing as that which compressed itself into the look with which she returned Gunter's mocking smile.

(My mind worked overtime. Fixby? ... Fixby? ... Fixby? ... The name rang bells. Then it came. *Detective Constable Fixby*. The young copper who had reached for immortality, and ended up floating on the waters of a canal basin.

Jesus!

Such was the size of the Daniel who had strolled into this particular den of lions. Such was the size of his bastardy. Such was the monumental arrogance of his amorality.

This was Paul Gunter.)

AND SOMETHING HAD TO BLOW!

Something like a sigh—part-sigh, part-moan—eased its way across the room. Sullivan raised the palm of his right hand, warningly, but without moving his hand from where it hung by his side. It stayed them ... but only just.

The woman—Paulette Fixby—breathed something. A movement of the lips which was less than a whisper; some inaudible obscenity aimed at Gunter ... something no person heard, but everybody sensed. Something which, except for a moment like this, she would have suffered torture and still refused to mouth.

Gunter mocked her with his gaze and brought the glass to his lips.

And it blew!

The table in front of me crashed as Raff hurled it aside and stood up.

Gwen Raff breathed, 'David ... don't!' but I doubt whether Raff heard her.

He walked towards the bar counter. He walked stiff-legged—as if he, too, was held rigid by leg-irons—and the wall of coppers parted to let him pass then, as he passed, closed behind him. He stopped at the bar counter and faced Gunter at a distance of less than a yard.

Gunter eyed him. Quietly. Contemptuously. With cynical and calm amusement.

He murmured, 'Ah ... the crazy man.'

From where I saw sitting—even from that distance—I could see Raff's jaw muscles bunch; could see the neck muscles tighten, like hawsers taking an impossible strain.

And murder was in Raff's eyes—stark, naked, don't-give-a-damn murder—as he stared into the face of his tormentor and, with his right hand, reached towards the bar counter. The fingers walked across the bar counter top. They found the soda water siphon. They crawled up the glass side of the siphon and curled around the spout and lever, at the top.

With snake-speed savagery Raff jerked the siphon to shoulder height, then brought it down onto the edge of the bar counter. The glass splintered and flew—glass heavy enough and razor sharp enough to be on par with plate—and the spilled soda water swam over the surface of the bar counter and made an expanding skin of tiny bubble-bursts spread and drip from the edge ... and Raff had the most deadly of all make-do-and-mend fighting tools held, and ready for use.

There was a movement, as the three heavies tried to muscle their way towards their paymaster, but the wall of forensic beef held them helpless.

Somebody—one of the watching women—sobbed, 'Oh, my God ... don't let him.'

Gunter looked slightly bored—slightly amused—and sipped at the whisky.

Then Raff spoke ... if that word can be used to describe the strangled croak which came from the back of his throat.

He said, 'Five seconds, Gunter. Five seconds! Then I use this. Into your face—at your eyes ... *hard*. Five seconds ... starting from now.'

Gunter looked past Raff, and at Sullivan.

He said, 'Is that legal, Sullivan? ... would you say?' and there wasn't the hint of a quaver in the tone.

'*One*,' ground Raff.

'Pick your men. Pick your rank,' said Sullivan in a flat voice. 'Any ten. They'll all climb into a witness box and swear you fell and cut yourself on a broken glass.'

The fat man—the copper Raff had identified as Lennox—eased himself a couple of feet along the bar and reached for the half pint of beer which Gunter had ordered as a chaser for the whisky.

'*Two*.'

Even from the room-width away I could see Raff tense himself for the thrust; could see the slight tremble of the sharded edge of the siphon.

The man from the local newsrag raised the viewfinder of his camera to his eye.

One of the heavies snarled, 'What the hell! You can't ...' then switched the words to a half-groan-half-gasp as a copper drove an elbow hard into his gut.

Gunter raised the glass to his lips—unhurriedly, deliberately —and drank some of the whisky.

'*Three.*'

There was a movement ... sudden, and split-second.

The flashbulb of the newshound's camera blasted eye-searing light and, simultaneously, half a pint of mild hit the lens of the camera.

Lennox eyed the empty glass ruefully, and murmured, 'Sorry, old son. I always was accident prone.'

'You bloody ...' began the newshound.

'Naughty!' warned Lennox, gently.

'*Four.*'

And nobody in the room doubted that, on the next count, Raff would mutilate Gunter for life. That the smashed siphon would slice its way into Gunter's face—perhaps blind him—and that the blood-letting would be sickening, and that Gunter (even Gunter!) would scream ... every man knew it, and the only man who didn't seem to give a damn was Gunter himself.

And every copper knew that, on the next count, there'd be the greatest, and the most dangerous, cover-up in the history of the Police Service ... and *they* didn't give a damn.

Gunter tipped the last of the whisky down his throat. Not quickly. Not slowly. But very deliberately—at a normal drinking speed—before he placed the glass on the bar counter top. He jerked a handkerchief from his breast pocket, dabbed his lips, then replaced the handkerchief. Again, not slowly, not quickly, but very deliberately.

'*Five.*'

Gunter was actually turning as Raff drew back his arm for the thrust. Sullivan caught Raff's elbow and Sugden (Lennox's pal) grabbed Raff's left arm as, in the space of an eye-blink. it became obvious that Gunter was leaving *The Woodchopper's Arms*. Raff struggled for a moment, then seemed to collapse; his fingers opened and the broken siphon fell onto the floor.

'Easy, David,' said Sullivan, gently. 'You backed him down.'

But it was a lie, and everybody (except, perhaps, Raff himself) recognised it as a lie. The victory (if there'd been a victory) had been Gunter's because Gunter had left the impression that he was leaving the pub because he wanted to leave the pub ... and that all the Raffs, and all the coppers, and all the broken soda water siphons in the world hadn't influenced his decision one way, or the other.

Sullivan growled, 'Let the other bastards follow him,' and the wall of coppers parted to allow the three heavies passage to the door, after their master.

The newshound was still wiping beer from his camera, when Lennox turned to him, grinned, and said, 'Hard luck, old son. It could have been a great picture.'

'You did it on purpose,' blazed the newshound. 'You threw that ...'

'It's a wicked world, sonny,' mused Lennox.

'But if you think, just because I didn't get a picture, I'm not ...'

'A wicked world,' repeated Lennox. 'For instance—I know your editor ... known him for donkey's years.'

'So?'

'He owes me a few favours.'

The newshound narrowed his eyes, and said, 'If you think ...'

'I never think, old son,' said Lennox, cheerfully. 'I always *know*. That, or keep my mouth shut. And I know you're out of a job if you even try to do what I think you have visions of doing. No crusading journalism—not this time ... eh? I wouldn't like it. Your editor wouldn't like it. None of the blokes here would like it. And even *you* wouldn't like it ... not after every copper in the Northern Union's trotted you off to court a couple of dozen times for everything short of breathing out of step. So-o, if you fancy yourself as a future Hannen Swaffer, forget the last five minutes—let me buy you a drink, instead ... eh?'

The newshound made a decision. (If you can call the choice he had a 'decision'. Lennox had him pinned up a one-way street; if he wanted a future, there was only one direction left. He was no glory boy. It damn near strangled him, but it was the only decision he could make.

He took a deep breath, blew out his cheeks, looked disgusted, then said, 'It'll cost you a triple whisky.'

'Cheap at the price, son.'

'And thanks ... for showing me just what they mean, when they call you people "pigs".'

Lennox grinned. I didn't know the man, but I knew his breed; and they are insult-proof.

He said, 'They love us, son. Who *doesn't* like a nice thick slice of home-cooked ham?'

Outside, a car started up and drove away.

Which meant ...?

We-ell, it meant that, despite everything—despite a pub filled to bursting point with angry coppers—despite just about every rank in the Police Service, all prepared to commit perjury—despite being within a whisker's breadth of being blinded and marked for life—Gunter had done what he'd set out to do ... and, having done it, walked away.

Jesus!

They should have fixed a wall plaque ... 'Paul Gunter Was Here'.

There was a presentation. There always is. Irregardless of how much, or how little, the man has been liked—how much, or how little, the man has contributed to law enforcement by making the Police Service his career—there is always a speech, followed by a presentation. The older hands (like myself) can gauge a man's reputation with his fellow coppers via the speech and (especially) via the thought given to, and the cost of, the present.

Collins's present was peculiar to him. It wasn't the usual pewter (sometimes, silver-plated) tankard ... 'And, when he uses it, I hope he spares a thought for his old colleagues, and the happy hours they had together.' It wasn't the uninspired and inevitable timepiece ... 'And, when he looks at it, or winds it up, I hope he spares a thought for his old colleagues—etc—etc —etc.' It wasn't the same old dreary, gimcrack table-lamp ... 'And when he switches it on, I hope—etc—etc—etc.'

This time, the present was different.

This time, Sullivan's speech was different and Collins's 'few words of thanks' were different ... because Gunter had forced them to be different.

Raff didn't hear them. Nor did Gwen Raff, nor Paulette Fixby. The three of them had left, shortly after Gunter; Gwen trying to calm her husband and comfort Fixby's widow, and failing on both counts. They'd left because to stay would have been a mockery and, after they'd gone, some of the men (and most of the women) had tried to kid themselves that what had happened had been little more than a minor annoyance; they'd poured a little more booze down their gizzards, wandered into the rear room to sample the cold buffet of paté sandwiches, crisps, cheese straws and what have you, then settled down for the presentation ceremony.

Sullivan made the speech and, at first, the normal platitudes had their regular airing but, gradually, steel entered into his voice and rime frost gathered on the surface of his eyes.

'... What we have witnessed, tonight—earlier this evening— has been far more than a get-together of friends. A farewell ram-sammy for a man we'll not only miss, but who we'll miss *as from tomorrow*. It's that—and that's what it was intended to be ... but it's turned out to be something much more than even that. Something which—speaking personally—makes me want to puke.

'Corruption, ladies and gentlemen. That's what the dem-onstration, earlier this evening, was about. Corruption ... and that a man can buy himself complete immunity from the law. Not tonight, of course! Tonight he didn't put a foot wrong. Because the people in this room can't be bought ... or, at least, I *hope* they can't be bought. They haven't yet *been* bought ... that's the main thing. Tonight he had to behave himself because, tonight he wasn't beyond the law. But we know—every man in this room knows—that without corruption, he wouldn't have come here, because he *couldn't* have come here. He'd be behind bars ... and Detective Constable Fixby's widow would not have had to sit there, and have her face rubbed in the dirt.

'Unfortunately ...' He sighed, then continued, 'Unfortunately we are held rigid by certain rules. The rules of law. Occasionally —it's an open secret—we break those rules, for the sake of common justice. When we do, we do it at our peril ... and this is as it should be, because we're coppers. We're guardians of the law, not makers of the law ... much less breakers of the law! But, by and large, we're decent men, not given to violence. We resist violence with counter-violence ... but that always gives the villain the first clout. And, after that first clout, if he can duck—or if somebody in high enough office is on the take— he gets away with it. And what happened here, tonight, is one result. Unfortunately—and despite what certain ill-informed members of the intelligentsia believe—we are not an organisation geared to vengeance ... but I sometimes wish we were ...'

All told it lasted for about five minutes, and Dick Sullivan surprised me; he was a man of action, rather than a man of talk ... but (as I found out) he could string words together when words were meant to say something.

The present was something Collins wanted. Something I knew he'd treasure. Something which would add pleasure to his life, and make even more perfect the only hobby he allowed himself.

A set of five, long-playing records, housed in a handsome presentation case; ten sides which, together, formed the complete sequence of Bach's Harpsichord Concertoes. Collins was a hi-fi fanatic, with one of the finest stereo set-ups in the district. Where other men loved women, Collins loved music ... and these records represented one more immaculate mistress he could take home, and claim as his own.

He accepted them with such obvious pleasure that, for a few moments, Gunter was forgotten. But not for long. Having said the standard 'thank you' noises, Collins eased himself into the territory already staked out by Sullivan.

'... And, as a small consolation for having had to suffer the

33

minor inconveniences of police life, I shall now be able to read all about the iniquities of certain people, happy in the knowledge that other men have the impossible task of checking their progress within the hampering confines of an otherwise near-perfect law ...'

That was all. The rest of the 'few words of appreciation' followed the usual pattern; not quite as many platitudes, but that only because Collins was old-fashioned enough to use the English language in a more precise manner that the average non-academic. Followed by *For He's a Jolly Good Fellow.* Followed by a loosening of corsets and a letting down of hair, as the booze made tongues wag and eased indiscretions from their hiding places.

Lennox, and his pal, left. Then Sullivan. Then, at half-past-ten, my taxi arrived and I shuffled my way towards the door.

Collins saw me leaving and accompanied me to the waiting cab.

When I'd wangled myself into the front passenger seat, and before he closed the door, Collins said, 'I'll be in touch, Charles ... soon. And I'm very glad indeed you could come.'

It was the way he used the words. The nuances which loaded what was an otherwise innocent and good-mannered remark with ...

With what?

Before I could ask, he'd closed the door, the driver had flipped the gear-stick and we were away.

Nights.

If the daytime merely soured me, the night brought on an active loathing. I hated the darkness, I hated the silence, I hated the loneliness.

Solitude ... God knows how much high-flown crap has been written about—talked about—that particular state. But always by people who had a choice. Those without a choice know (and have always known) the hard truth and the dividing line; that solitude is a self-imposed loneliness, and a loneliness which can

34

be ended when it becomes a burden. But loneliness is loneliness, and can never be mistaken for solitude, because true loneliness is without end and without beauty.

Loneliness is a silent curse and, at night (and without Elaine) I was a much-cursed man.

My home was a bungalow, for obvious reasons ... and for a couple of not-so-obvious reasons. I could get around, as long as I didn't have stairs to cope with. And (prior to Elaine dying) we'd always lived in houses. After the crippling, I'd slept in a downstairs room ... but the downstairs room of a three-storeyed *house*.

Moving into the bungalow had meant getting rid of furniture; more than half the furniture. I'd given it away. My daughter, Susan, and her husband had had first choice, then the rest had gone to friends ... real friends who'd understood all my reasons.

One moronic bastard (a man I wouldn't have let touch so much as a clothes peg) had expressed surprise. Why didn't I sell what I didn't want?

What an idiot question!

The thought of *selling* it—'our' home ... Jesus!

It would have been like putting Elaine up for auction.

However ...

I moved into the bungalow which (I kidded myself) would ease the hurt a little, because we'd always lived in houses. I parted with much of the furniture which (again, I kidded myself) would make the memories less liable to jump out from dark corners when I wasn't expecting them.

(I was a great one for kidding myself, in those days.)

The bungalow I chose was next-door to nowhere, and this (again) for obvious reasons. The one thing I could live without was *neighbourliness*. Stuff neighbourliness I didn't want some simpering biddy making a bloody nuisance of herself by doing her good deed for the day around my midden. I was self-sufficient. I could look after myself ... I'd damn-all else with which to occupy my mind. I could brew tea and I could fry eggs. I could also read ... therefore, the flashier aspects of the culinary art would come with practice.

That was the big idea, and it almost worked ... and that the 'almost' bit is the most important piece of all is something I had to live and learn.

Nevertheless ... no regrets. I may not be a complete man, but I am an independent man. I may not be a happy man, but I do not (partly because I *cannot*) impose my misery upon my fellow-men.

I comfort myself by counting what few blessings I still have. But at night! ... at night, blessings are very hard to find.

By midnight, I'd worked my way between the sheets, Susan had phoned me (a nightly exchange of greetings and news; Susan's idea, and something which had become part of my pattern of living) and I was in the darkness listening to the radio ... listening, but *not* listening, because the pop stuff churned out by the B.B.C. at that hour is not my personal idea of entertainment. The occasional tune came over (the occasional *tune*, as opposed to guitar-backed noise) and some of the tunes were oldies, played by men who knew music but, as the night grew older, the pearls became fewer and the garbage became thicker and, at last, I pushed myself into a half-sitting position, switched on the bedside lamp, turned the radio onto cassette-player and tried a spot of Gilbert and Sullivan for size.

It usually worked. And why not? ... the combination of satirical words and satirical music is as perfect a union as you're ever likely to get.

The Mikado. Somebody once described it as 'the Hamlet of the Savoy Operas' ... and it's a damn good description. Normally, and before the male section of the chorus have introduced themselves as 'gentlemen of Japan' the real-life stupidities of the world have been elbowed aside by the make-believe stupidities of Titipu.

But not that night.

That night, I was restless. At first, I put my discomfort down to a point (about the size of an old-fashioned sixpence) in my spine, at the small of my back; a point below which feeling

36

ended. Periodically, it pained me. Not bad—not unbearably, you understand—but rather like the first warning twinge of oncoming toothache. Indeed, to call it *pain* is, itself an over-statement. It is more in the nature of a warning of pain ... even the *hope* of pain, when it is first encountered. A false hope, as I lived to learn but, because of its falseness, an irritation. A nuisance ... one more tiny nuisance to add to the magnificent nuisance of being half-dead!

Ordinarily, I could bear it. I could ignore it—pretend it wasn't there—and, by so doing, banish it and, with it, the lying promise of a return of feeling.

But not that night. That night, I could not dismiss it, any more than I could concentrate upon the splendour of the D'Oyly Carte performance.

That night, I could only remember Collins's retirement party ... and Raff ... and Fixby's widow ... and (but most of all) Paul Gunter.

After about half an hour, I muttered, 'The hell with it!' switched off the cassette-player and hauled myself out of bed and into my wheelchair.

(My secret ... a secret which, by this time, you have solved. That, in the privacy of the bungalow, I sometimes use a wheelchair. It saved time and the fiddling around with straps and braces, before the leg-irons could be fixed into position. I hated that bloody wheelchair and, each time I used it, I sent a silent apology to Elaine ... because *she* wouldn't have allowed me to use it.

She'd have seen me crawl, first.

But I used the wheelchair that night.)

I brewed coffee. Black and strong. I lighted a pipe. Then sipped coffee, smoked my pipe and tried to untangle the maze of mixed-up thoughts which were knotted together under my skull.

For example ... coppers.

Show me a good copper, and I'll show you a man who could have been a big-time crook. 'Sullivan, Raff, Collins ... men I knew personally. Metcalfe, of the West Riding, Gosling of the Met., Hoover of the F.B.I.—legendary policemen ... and thank God for that. Because any one of them (and any one of a score of other, similar men) could have made the Kray Firm look like a vicarage tea-party.

They just happen to have landed on the right side of the fence—*our* side ... that's all.

And don't let the I-think-your-policemen-are-wonderful con fool you. The choice of nine-hundred-and-ninety-nine coppers in every thousand has damn-all to do with 'vocation', and not one hell of a lot to do with law-enforcement. They become coppers for other reasons; less obvious and, sometimes, less honourable reasons ... and some of the scum rise to the top, and that for no better reason than that they *are* scum.

Okay—I am now tearing the wings from the butterfly ... I tore them off that night, after Collins's party, when even Gilbert and Sullivan couldn't shoo away the bogey-men. But, having torn them off, I inspected them very closely and, eventually, learned exactly how the butterfly worked.

Let me tell you ...

I enjoyed bobbying because bobbying gave me power. I could detain a fellow-creature against his will ... and for no better reason than that he wouldn't answer a question I'd no right to ask. I could brain-wash him into admitting a crime ... and, here and there, a crime he hadn't committed. If he was a big enough villain, and if he resisted violently enough, I could kill him ... and earn a commendation for my murder.

That (skimmed of all its high-flown hogwash) is why I enjoyed bobbying. Nor am I inhuman or unique, because that is the reason why most coppers enjoy bobbying. Because it gives them power.

They may not misuse that power—most of them don't— but it's *there* ... and, as always, power corrupts.

Not fiscal corruption. Mental corruption. I have known coppers who, throughout their whole service, have never taken a brass farthing as a back-hander ... and every one of them mentally corrupted to hell and beyond. Every one of them with a skull packed tight with 'Them-and-Us' beliefs. Every one of them rotten with the worm of arrogance. Every one of them incapable of the simple human failing of being wrong.

I know. I was one of them ... until a bullet nicked my spine.

Until that night, after Collins's 'do', when I couldn't sleep, and I sat in a wheelchair, smoked my pipe and allowed my mind to toy with certain previously forbidden thoughts.

For example ... thoughts about coppers.

For example ... thoughts about crooks.

So—I ask you—what is a crook? Who is a criminal, and who is not a criminal? You should know—you, of all people—therefore, answer me ... even though I will not hear your answer. Answer me, and I will be satisfied, because the thought which must be given to the answer is, itself, answer enough.

The little man, who filches a tin of pears from the shelf of the supermarket? Is *he* a criminal? Oh, he's a felon—that, I know ... but is he a *criminal*? And, if so, why not the arms-dealer who sells his products to some tin-pot dictatorship, knowing that they will be used to slaughter innocent women and kids? Why should one end up with a 'previous conviction', and the other end up with a knighthood?

The guy who pushes his accelerator a fraction of an inch too far down? Who breaks some man-imposed speed limit? Is *he* a criminal? ... he's certainly broken the (so-called) Criminal Law. If so, why not the guy who designed some super-sonic jet and who, because he fed some equally fractionally incorrect data into the complex, but unthinking, brain of a computer, is the man basically responsible for a future breath-stopping air disaster? Why should one be fined, while the other is honoured?

Can you see sense in it, friend?

I'm damned if *I* can!

But this I know—this truth I dragged out of myself, that night when I couldn't sleep, but couldn't stop thinking—that crime is only what *we* call crime; that everything up to, and including, murder and treason, can be excused (can even be applauded) if the reasons are right ... and that the rightfulness (even the righteousness) of those reasons is governed, not by human suffering, but by the conveniences of society and economic pressures.

But coppers don't think that way, do they? Coppers aren't *allowed* to think that way ... which (I suppose) is what I mean when I talk of 'mental corruption'.

Which is why you will never—no matter how hard you look, no matter how many law libraries you search through—you will *never* find a satisfactory definition of the very reason for a Police Service ... *crime*.

My pipe was cold, the coffee was scummed and, beyond the windows, dawn was making silhouettes of the trees. I'd spent the whole night pounding my brains to pulp, and for no good purpose. I still hadn't any clear-cut answers—I wasn't even sure what the hell the questions were, any more—and I almost began to wish I'd given *The Woodchopper's Arms* a miss.

I trundled myself to the bathroom, turned on the taps and, while the bath was filling, wriggled out of my pyjamas. Getting into the bath was (as always) something of a gymnastic exercise, despite the arrangement of bars with which I could haul, higher and lower myself, but the sudded water was cleansing, and it seemed to cleanse the soul and the mind, as well as the body.

An hour and a half later, it was morning, and I was dried and dressed (complete with leg-irons and elbow crutches), running an electric razor over my cheeks and ready to face another dreary day of pseudo-activity.

And, brother, was I mistaken!

Collins rang at about eleven/eleven-thirty.

Was I busy? ... *me*—busy!

If not, would I do him a favour? Would I have lunch with him?

It was important—very important—and he'd appreciate it, if I could come along.

Did I know *The Silver Bowl Restaurant,* in Cowling Arcade? Would one o'clock be convenient?

I said 'Yes' and 'No' in all the right places, replaced the receiver, wondered what the hell had put urgency into Collins's tone, then dialled the local taxi firm and arranged for them to pick me up at twelve-thirty.

The Silver Bowl was a good restaurant; and, by that, I mean good ... not merely 'nice'. The prices were high enough to scare the quick-snack crowd clear into the next county, but what you paid for you got. Service; the waiters didn't 'hover'; they did their job, and did it well, then disappeared but (via some extra-sensory mysticism, known only to themselves) were around and ready whenever they were needed. Cleanliness; and, by that I do not mean a quick brush-and-crumb-tray job; there wasn't even dust-motes, much less dirt, and the soft, background hum of strategically placed extractor fans kept the air from becoming anything other than pure. The food was what food is meant to be, but rarely is; a mite exotic for my simple taste, perhaps but (for the sake of experience) I was prepared to try scampi cock-tails, followed by casserole of partridge with red wine and mushrooms—complete with all the necessary trimmings ... if only because it made a change from fish and chips!

You will (I hope) appreciate that the restaurant was chosen by Collins; that the choice typified Collins's taste for excellence ... that *The Silver Bowl* was chosen, quite naturally, because he *was* Collins.

Much of the eating area was divided into partitioned alcoves; each alcove a tiny, isolated cell of absolute privacy.

The manager guided me to one of the alcoves.

Collins was already there as, also, was Raff. I hadn't expected Raff, but I was not dismayed. I liked the man. We had much in common; one of the things being that we'd both been high-ranking coppers (he in the city force, I in the county) before the job had broken us ... each in a different way.

Collins was sipping a pink gin. A watered-down whisky, with broken ice floating on its surface, was on the table, in front of Raff. I ordered a lager, before I eased myself into the alcove and onto one of the cushioned benches.

Raff looked ill; deadly ill. His face had the colour of bleached parchment and (even since the night before) his eyes seemed to have sunk deeper into their sockets ... sockets which were shadowed, and made even darker by the contrasting whiteness of his face.

Until the waiter placed the lager in front of me, and left, we talked inconsequentialities; the weather, last night's party, the latest political cock-up ... words which, added together, fell a long way short of conversation.

Then there was a silence, as if each was waiting for the other to speak.

Raff reached out a hand, turned the glass slowly, and spoke to the whisky.

He said, 'Paulette's dead.'

'Paulette?'

'Paulette Fixby.'

Three sentences ... five words. A question sandwiched between two dead-voiced statements. Not much. The way I tell it, it isn't much. Come to think of it, it *wasn't* much; no histrionics, no raised voices, not even a frown or a scowl. Just five flat, uninteresting words. ('How's the weather?' 'What?' 'How's the weather?' ... that sort of an exchange.)

Collins said, 'David phoned me, earlier this morning. I thought we should get together.'

'Oh, sure.' I didn't know what the hell to say—or what the hell I meant—so I repeated, 'Oh, sure.'

Raff sipped at the whisky; not a real drink, just a moistening of dry lips. Then he lowered the glass, placed it gently on the table and began to run a forefinger around its rim. Slowly ... at about the same speed at which he spoke. And gently ... as gently as his voice was soft. His brow furrowed as he talked; as if what he was saying was something he hadn't previously heard. As if he was mildly surprised.

42

He said, 'She lives near. Paulette, I mean. They're friends—good friends ... Gwen and Paulette. Were. They were great friends. Last night—she was upset ... y'know, upset. I mean—y'know ... she would be, wouldn't she? She—er—she came to our place for a couple of hours. Y'know ... till she got over the worst. We—er—we wanted her to stay the night. Gwen asked her. But she wouldn't ... she said she'd prefer to go home.

'Gwen went, this morning. Y'know ... to see if she'd slept okay. They were—sorry, I've already said—they were great friends. And—and there was this smell of gas. Even at the door. The front door ... even there, you could get a whiff of it. It must have—must have been on all night. Damn near all night.'

He stopped the movement of his forefinger, but left the finger resting gently on the rim of the glass. He raised his head, and looked at my face as he continued speaking. And, as he spoke, tears built up and spilled from his eyes. One tear from each eye; huge, heartbroken tears which gathered along the edge of the lower lids, grew fat then toppled over to roll down his cheeks.

He said, 'She'd—she'd had a bath. Ch-changed her clothes ... all the way to the skin. And—and a clean nightdress. She—she left a note. Apologising. Y'know—*apologising* ... for all the trouble she was going to cause. Then—then the hearthrug, in front of the gas fire. With her head on a pillow. And—and—Jesus!—she'd even crossed her hands across her breasts ... to—to save somebody having to do even *that*. I mean—I mean ... Oh, my Christ! The poor bitch. The poor, poor bitch.'

'Aye.' I nodded, but still didn't know what the hell to say. I wanted to share Raff's misery thinking, maybe that, by sharing it, I could ease some of it from his own aching shoulders. I wanted to do that, but I was damned if I knew how. So I murmured, 'The poor bitch', and hoped he understood and believed that I meant it.

I looked across at Collins.

Collins was fitting a cigarette into a briar holder. He was concentrating all his attention upon this tiny task; being fiddling and old-womanish. Then, when the cigarette was in the holder to his liking, he took a lighter from his pocket, lighted the cigarette, inhaled smoke and returned the lighter to his pocket. He took his time. Every part of the whole sequence of events was separate, deliberate and concluded before the start of the next.

And yet ...

How the hell can I explain it? It would need a Tolstoy, or a Dylan Thomas, to put it into good words. To give the feeling which was there, and invisible; invisible, but as obvious—and as obvious to the eye—as Blackpool illuminations. Abstract but, at the same time, as solid as reinforced concrete.

Understand me, it was not hatred. I doubt if a man like Collins is ever capable of animal-mad, mind-blowing hatred. I doubt if he knows the feel of such an emotion.

And yet loathing was there ... loathing and disgust.

Imagine a man; somebody born to excellence. Imagine him at some five-star hotel, turning down the bed-linen and finding a cockroach between the sheets. Imagine his feelings, and his outrage ... and you are almost there.

You are at least within sight of what Collins felt, and of what I could see and what I could feel emanating from him.

Did I say 'see'?

That, too, is an exaggeration. There was nothing—*nothing*—about his expression, or about the movement of his hands, to give evidence of what I knew was there. The deliberation of his movements, perhaps? The hint of a tightening at the mouth corners? Something about the eyes? ... an absence of the normal tranquility?

Or, maybe I'm kidding myself. Maybe this is all hindsight. Maybe I'm being very wise, after a pretty important event.

Nevertheless, it was there—the loathing and the disgust ... that much, at least, is not imagination.

Collins raised a hand, removed the holder from his mouth, and murmured, 'I think we'll order ... shall we?'

We ate. We ate in silence. We talked about nothing. We worked our way through scampi cocktails, and casserole of partridge with red wine and mushrooms, and we used our mouths for that, and that only.

44

The service was excellent. The wine was fine (although I am no connoisseur of wine) and the atmosphere of *The Silver Bowl* was both calming and insidious.

We could, if we required, talk. The choice was ours to make and, that we didn't talk, was the choice we made. Nevertheless, we *could* talk, if that was what we required. The privacy was complete and absolute; the partitions were sound-proof; the waiters were all deaf mutes; nothing we said could ever be overheard—could ever be repeated—could ever be passed on.

That was the atmosphere which gradually built up, as the three of us ate an excellent meal in a first-class restaurant.

The waiter cleared the last of the plates, and his fellow placed coffee-cups in front of us.

'Black or white, sir?'

'Black, please,' said Collins, quietly.

'Black or white, sir?'

'Eh?' Raff blinked, then looked up at the waiter.

'Black or white, sir?' repeated the waiter, patiently.

'Oh—er—black ... black.'

'Black or white, sir?'

'White,' I said.

'Brandy, sir?' asked the waiter.

'Not for me, thank you.' Collins glanced enquiringly at Raff and myself.

Raff muttered, 'No ... no thanks.'

'No brandy,' I growled.

The waiter did a quick, half-bow and disappeared to his own little hiding place, and we spooned sugar into our coffees.

Collins threaded a new cigarette into his holder, lighted it, then spoke.

He glanced at us, each in turn, then drawled, 'We're agreed, I take it, that something must be done about Gunter?'

'Are we?' The surprise on my face was carried through into the question.

'You agreed to this get-together, Charles,' he said, quietly.

'I agreed to join you for lunch,' I corrected him. 'I accepted an invitation ... but there was no mention of Gunter.'

45

'For Christ's sake, Charlie! You're not ...'

'Charles.' Collins gestured Raff into silence. 'You witnessed what happened last night?'

'I did.' I nodded.

'With disapproval, I hope?'

'What do *you* think?'

'The man has murdered a police officer ... every policeman in that room knew it.'

'Aye.'

'More than that, even. Gunter *knew* that every policeman in that room knew it.'

'David made him ...' I began.

'David did nothing,' interrupted Collins, smoothly. 'Nothing! David did what Gunter allowed him to do. You know—I know —every man in that room, including David—knows that Sullivan would not have allowed David to use the broken siphon on Gunter's face.'

'Maybe,' I conceded.

'Charles, you know.' Collins smiled, politely. 'Sullivan was bluffing ... and the bluff was merely backed by every other policeman present. The only man who *wasn't* bluffing was David ... but David wouldn't have been allowed to do what he was threatening to do. It was too far outside the law. Policemen may not stand by and watch an Unlawful Wounding. It isn't allowed. It's an utterly impossible proposition ... surely?'

'Aye.' The admission wasn't easy to make, but I made it. 'You could be right.'

'I *am* right.'

'All right ... you're right. But ...'

'Doesn't it mean anything to you?' Life showed in Raff's face, for the first time since I'd arrived at the restaurant. Not very nice life—furious life; life spawned from a soul-tearing rage ... but life, nevertheless. His voice was a soft snarl, as he said, 'Doesn't it mean *anything*? That the bastard can kill a copper, and walk around boasting of it? That he can drive his victim's wife to suicide? ... and still walk the streets? That he can ...'

'David ... please!'

Once again, Collins silenced Raff. Then Collins sipped at his

46

coffee—quite calmly, quite casually—before he rested his forearms on the table, leaned forward and talked directly at me.

He said, 'Charles—in order that you may have no misconceptions—let me spell it out for you. Let me explain the problem. Then, let me outline the only possible solution.'

'It might help,' I growled, sardonically.

Collins paused to draw on his cigarette, before continuing.

'The subject under discussion,' he said, 'is Paul Gunter. He is the reason for this lunch. He is the reason why we three are together, this afternoon.'

'I didn't know that.'

'You now know.' Collins treated me to one of his slow, master-to-pupil smiles. 'Paul Gunter considers himself a man well beyond the reach of the law. He can—or so he thinks—murder policemen with impunity. He can—or so he thinks—walk into public houses, mock the widows of the policemen he has murdered and, by so doing, drive them to suicide ... and with equal impunity. Paul Gunter thinks he can do these things ... agreed?'

I hesitated before I answered but, when I did answer, I spoke only the truth.

I said, 'No—I don't agree ... Paul Gunter *can* do these things.'

Collins nodded, slowly. As if accepting as valid the correction to the previous remark.

'He can,' he agreed, softly. 'But only because the law allows him to. Only because the law requires hard evidence before it inflicts punishment. Only because—as Richard so succinctly put it, last night—the Police Service is not a vehicle for vengeance. As far as Paul Gunter is concerned, these are social weaknesses. He hides behind them. He commits crime ... then cocks a snook at what decent people would call "justice".'

'Bully for Paul Gunter,' I murmured.

'You don't mean that, Charles.'

'No—maybe I don't ... not quite like that,' I agreed, reluctantly. 'But I'll tell you what I *do* mean. And—like you—I'll spell it out ... if necessary.'

'Please do. I'm interested.'

This time, it was my turn to sip coffee, before I spoke. This

47

time it was my turn to put my elbows on the table, lean forward and talk into somebody's face.

'Henry,' I said, 'I don't know how much money you've got but, unless you hold major shares in General Motors, forget it. In your own academic language, you're talking about fixing Gunter. And there's only one way of fixing that particular comedian ... and that's *via* a fix. It means buying your way through to somebody—one of his immediate henchmen—who's near enough to either nark, or put the finger on his own boss. *It can't be done.* They've all been leaned upon ... and by experts. They've all had their collars grabbed. They've been thrown inside —they've been roughed up—you name it ... it's happened. And none of them—not one of them—has ever dropped Gunter. He rules them. He dominates them. He's un-fixable. And, even if he wasn't—even if he *could* be fixed ...'

I stopped talking, and scowled down at my coffee.

'Yes?' encouraged Collins, gently.

'You're a copper,' I muttered.

'Not any more.'

'Coppers don't do things that way ... not those that aren't bent.'

'I stopped being a policeman, at midnight,' said Collins, slowly.

'So?'

'I can now do things I could not do, as a policeman. Things I would have liked to have done, but couldn't ... and now *can*.'

'You're out of your skull ... both of you!' It wasn't an explosion, but it was certainly a minor bore of anger. These two idiots were my friends; old friends and valued friends. I'd known them years—more years than *that*—and, until this moment, I'd counted them as sane and level-headed men. And now this! This crack-handed, lunatic, half-cocked scheme for dotting Gunter in the goolies. And Collins, of all people! 'What the hell do you think you are?' I snapped. 'Some sort of real-life, latter-day "Four Just Men"? Where the bloody hell d'you think it'll get you both? I'll tell you. I'll tell you just where. In the nick ... that's where. Both of you. And for one hell of a long stretch. Gunter ... he'll play ping-pong with you. The pair of you. He has the organisation.

He has the money. He has the pull. He has everything! You try to work a fix on Paul Gunter and—I swear—he'll get *you*.'

'We do not,' drawled Collins, 'want to "work a fix" on him, Charles.'

'What the hell! You just said ...'

'We want to kill him.'

'As slowly as possible,' added Raff.

So-o ... with friends like that, who needs to know lunatics?

I wanted no part of it. Okay—I, too, hated Gunter. Okay—I, too, would cheerfully have served him, with a lemon in his mouth and sizzling hot with French fried vegetables. Okay—for my money, too, they should have thrown him away, and kept the afterbirth.

Nobody hated Paul Gunter more than I hated Paul Gunter. Not Collins. Not even Raff. But—Christ Almighty!—I knew my limitations. I knew *their* limitations ... which is more than they did!

Paul Gunter was like a cancer. He was around, and he'd stay around until the Almighty called 'Time's up', at which point Paul Gunter would have to row even his boat to the landing stage. But the boat itself was unsinkable ... but those two berks, Collins and Raff, didn't know it.

I mean—be fair ... two grown men—two middle-aged men—and, more than that, two ex-senior coppers—quietly discussing crime over coffee. Quietly discussing murder, for God's sake!

I would have left. I would have got up, and walked out ... had I been able. But the flaming taxi wasn't due to collect me until three o'clock, and it had started to rain (one of those hit-and-run early summer soakers) and I was damned if I was going to stand on the pavement, like a buckshee lamp-post waiting for a stray dog, in that lot.

Which meant I had to sit there, and listen.

And it was some conversation!

It was pure, unadulterated crap. It was concentrated bullshit. And that neither of them could recognise it for what it was staggered me. The subject-matter was homicide, and the suggestions for slaughtering Paul Gunter were as unlimited as they were unconstrained. From poisoning, to planting a home-made bomb under the bonnet of his car. From a blunt instrument across the back of his skull, to a rifle bullet between his eyes.

It takes one hell of a lot to shock me, but (I swear) I was shocked.

My own contribution to the crazy tête-á-tête was a periodic 'For Christ's sake!' which was politely ignored.

Understand me, they weren't outraged. Neither of them criticised my decision to be included out, as far as the elimination of Gunter was concerned. It was my decision—I made it ... they didn't argue. They thought I was wrong. They *said* I was wrong ... but without rancour.

Then they just went right ahead, and planned murder, while I sat there and listened.

The taxi arrived, on the dot. Collins strolled with me to the street and, as I worked my way onto the rear seat, he smiled.

He said, 'If you change your mind, Charles.'

'That,' I said, 'is not likely.'

'But, if you *do*. We'll be grateful.'

I leaned forward, stared up at him, and said, 'Henry—for the last time—don't be such a blazing fool. You ... you, of all people. David—okay—I can understand ... I *think* I can understand. He's a nice guy, but ...'

I moved my hands, palm-upwards. The gesture said what I didn't like to say.

'He's not mad,' insisted Collins.

'Y'know what?' I said, sadly. 'The way you've talked, this afternoon. Both of you ... I think you're *both* mad.'

It worried me. Hell, it worried me ... and that is the understatement of all time.

They were heading, full-throttle, for disaster. They were committing slow-motion suicide. And the stupid thing was, they didn't know it. They couldn't see ... because they refused to open their eyes.

Let me tell you ...

You cannot commit murder as easily as that. Not in this fair isle. We have a police force, second to none and, although the big gangs can, for a while, commit every crime up to, and including, butchery, there is a wall beyond which even *they* cannot go. And, if you seek confirmation, ask the Messinas—ask the Richardsons—ask the Krays. When they kill their own kind, the cops ask around—they go through the motions—but, having hosed the blood from the paving-stones, who cares? That offal becomes carrion-meat takes the skin from nobody's nose. It is more important that the nearest traffic snarl-up be untangled.

Okay—this is something the cops know ... something the wide-eyed innocents must never be told. Nevertheless, it is a law, within a law ... no, *outside* a law. It is (if you like) gangland's own law, and the cops allow them to enforce it, but strictly within the boundaries of gangland itself. Scum may kill scum, with comparative immunity ... just as long as it doesn't get into a habit.

But that's all!

Let them touch non-scum—let them harm one hair of an innocent by-stander—and the boom comes down with a wallop that shakes the earth.

Which is fine, as far as it goes. A thing of checks and balances; a set of rules, unwritten but inviolable. That fish eat fish, and that the sharks come out on top. But let one of the sharks be gaffed—let one to the top gang-bosses be knocked off—and, again, the boom comes down faster than gravity can pull it.

Why?

We-ell—that size of killing could lead to gang-war ... it *has* been known! Because, basically, we are dealing with mugs. Louts who are incapable of thought ... and a hell of a lot of them are corpse-happy. Their boss gets chopped and, without an atom of proof—without the ghost of anything remotely resembling evidence—they decide who's responsible, and chop back. Then, the pot boils over and innocent people get badly scalded.

So-o ... the boom comes down.

I knew these simple facts of constabulary life. So (presumably) did Collins and Raff. Which, in turn, meant that when they stiffened Gunter—*if* they stiffened Gunter—they wouldn't have a prayer. The jacks would dig, and dig deep and, eventually, nail them. Then the judge ...

Jesus! With two ex-top-rankers, he'd slam them inside and melt the key.

Which, in turn, made me worried ... *bloody* worried.

All that late-afternoon, I tried my usual remedies for the blues.

I flicked through all the T.V. channels and, for my trouble, was given a choice of highbrow crap I didn't understand or lowbrow crap imported as 'comedy' from America. I tried the radio; a play I didn't want to know, stratospheric chamber music or a mouthy goon cracking corny jokes between caterwauling 'pop' ... what a choice! I thumbed my way through the cassettes and, eventually, plumped for Rudolph Serkin playing Beethoven's '*Pathetique*' ... mainly because Ludwig van must have been in the mood I was in when he wrote that first movement.

Except I couldn't set it to music.

I toyed with certain ideas. To ring Gwen Raff, and warn her of her husband's latest lunacy. (No good. David Raff was the world's most obstinate pig-head. I knew it. Gwen Raff knew it. Phoning her would only add *her* worries to my own.) To ring Susan, and ask if *she* could come up with any brainwaves. (Again, no good. Susan was my daughter, and I loved her dearly, but she was also the wife of my son-in-law, and my son-in-law was Christopher Tallboy—and Christopher Tallboy was a very good detective sergeant. He was in my old county constabulary ... which—okay meant that he was not part of Henry and David's old mob. But he was a good copper. Which was enough. Because, Susan being Susan, she wouldn't be able to *not* tell her husband. And Chris being Chris, he wouldn't be able to *not* pass on the info to Dick Sullivan. Very involved ... a very involved way of making Henry Collins and David Raff joint owners of a man-sized manure-dump.)

I wished to hell Elaine was around.

She'd have known. She'd have worked it out for me. There was a solution—there's a solution to everything, if you're wise enough—and she'd have found it.

Me?

All I could do was sit there, listen to Beethoven's '*Pathetique*' and worry myself out of my skull.

I was a dummy. I couldn't walk ... let's not split hairs, for the sake of polite sympathy, the way I moved from Point 'A' to Point 'B' could not be described as *walking*. I couldn't think ... two of my closest mates were due to dive, head first, into a vat of boiling oil and I couldn't think of one damn thing to do to stop them.

I was the most useless—the most lonely—bastard on the face of Mother Earth.

It was about five o'clock when I came up with the answer. An answer, of a sort ... but the best I could think of. Cut out Susan, cut out Chris and go straight to Dick Sullivan, direct.

I could talk to him. He, too, was a friend. He was also Henry Collins's friend and David Raff's friend.

Off the record—strictly off the record—he might be able to help. He might be able to put the skids under them (unofficially) before they hit the slope and gathered too much speed to be stopped.

I phoned his home and spoke to his wife, Mary. She said she expected him back before six. I told her it was urgent; that I wanted to see him; that what I had to say couldn't be said over the telephone; that I'd wait up—however late it was—until he arrived.

Mary said she'd tell him, and I thanked her.

She asked me how I was, and I told her I was fine. She said she was glad; she pretended to believe me, even though she knew I was a liar. I liked Mary Sullivan. I liked her a lot—she reminded me of Elaine ... she could spot a liar before he'd cleared the horizon. But she knew when to make-believe that a lie was the truth.

He arrived at the bungalow at a few minutes going up to twelve. Late; closing to midnight, and later than I'd expected.

He started to apologise.

I said, 'Forget it, Dick. Day? Night? What the hell difference does it mean to *me*?'

'Still, if Mary hadn't said it was urgent ...'

'You've come, that's the main thing.'

I settled him in an easy chair, with a beer and tobacco for his pipe, then left him for the kitchen.

What I had in mind was a little like platting spider's web into a tow-rope; this boy was more than a serving cop, he was also an assistant chief constable. Assistant Chief Constable (Crime). Nor was he bent—or even slightly curved ... they just didn't come straighter than Dick Sullivan.

And, what I was going to ask him was ...

We-ell—maybe not illegal. But the words 'Conspiracy to Murder' can cover one hell of an acreage, and is only one small step short of the real thing. Could be that Collins and Raff had already *committed* a crime; merely by waving stupid ideas around in *The Silver Bowl Restaurant*. I wasn't sure ... except that a good lawyer could have argued a case in favour. I wasn't even one-hundred-per-cent sure of Dick Sullivan, because if *he* argued a case in favour of 'Conspiracy to Murder' I was wasting my time. I was sunk. And so, come to that, were Collins and Raff.

Hence the omelet.

I've already said—two years previously I could just about boil water ... but I'd had to learn. I'd taught myself how to cook simple dishes, and one of the masterpieces of my short, gastronomic repertoire was a little number which the cook-book called *Omelette au Jambon*. Ham and eggs, done up fancy, to you.

The omelet mix was ready in the dish. The cooked ham was already diced. I turned the gas-rings to medium heat, put one

54

large and one small frying pan on each ring, and slapped in the butter.

I could do it, too.

One of the kitchen walls was near enough to the cooker to give me a back-rest; I could prop myself against it, forget the elbow crutches, and have free use of my hands and arms. I'd long ago positioned a Formica-topped table within range and the *Omelette au Jambon* bits and pieces were arranged on this table. The diced ham ... ready to be tossed around in one of the pans of melted butter. The mixture of eggs, a little water, salt and freshly milled pepper ... ready for the butter in the other pan to colour to a pale fawn.

Nothing could go wrong ... nor did it.

Five minutes later I hobbled back into the main room, guiding a dumb-waiter with the front of my thighs and, on the dumb-waiter were two plates, each of which held a perfectly cooked diced-ham omelet.

Sullivan looked surprised.

He pushed himself up from the chair and took over the driving of the dumb-waiter.

He said, 'Look—I didn't expect you to ...'

'It's nothing,' I said, modestly. 'A quick snack. To go with the beer.'

'Yes, I know. But ...'

'And to prove I'm not just a pretty face.'

He grinned his friendship, positioned the dumb-waiter and waited for me to settle in the other easy chair.

From then on, and for the next fifteen minutes or so, it was cold beer and hot omelet ... and very tasty, too. I suppose we talked but, I can't remember what we said; something trivial—something unimportant—as Sullivan waited for whatever it was I wanted to see him about ... and as I *made* him wait, until the food and drink worked a mellowing effect upon a man from whom I was due to ask one hell of a favour.

It was well past midnight—almost thirty minutes into a new day—before the real talk began. We'd eaten, we were each tasting our second can of beer and both of us had pipes newly-packed and drawing well.

Sullivan settled back in his chair, eyed me questioningly, and said, 'What is it, then?'

'Mary told you it was urgent,' I fenced, warily. 'That's why I'm here.'

'It is ... *very* urgent.' I watched his face, as I added, 'And very unofficial.'

He waited. He knew something was coming, and he was far too old a dog to make rash promises before knowing precisely what it was he was letting himself in for.

'It's about Gunter,' I offered, invitingly.

'Paul Gunter?'

'Uhu.' I nodded.

'Something about Gunter? That's urgent? But—er—unofficial?' he mused. 'That makes it interesting, Charlie.'

'But unofficial,' I insisted.

'I wouldn't know.' He smiled a quick, twisted smile. 'If you mean you want your name kept out of it ...'

'No. Not that.'

'We-ell ...' He sipped at his beer. 'Information. That's what you're peddling ... right?'

'Aye. More, or less.'

'Information likely to help us nail Gunter?'

'No. Not that.'

'That's the only information I'm interested in, Charlie.'

I paused to keep abreast with him in the beer-drinking stakes, took a moment or two to choose my words, then said, 'You want Gunter out of the way. Right?'

'Right,' he agreed.

'At what cost?'

'Name your price. You know the rate of exchange for informants. If it's too ...'

'I'm not a bloody informant,' I snapped, irritably.

'I believe you ... so don't act like one.'

'It's ...' I swallowed, then said, 'Somebody's planning to kill Gunter.'

'Somebody?' He cocked a quizzical eyebrow.

'Somebody we both know,' I amplified.

'Rumour?' he asked. 'Or do you have evidence?'

56

'More than rumour. A lot more than rumour.'

'You're on thin ice, Charlie,' he warned, gently. 'A murder's planned, and you're pussyfooting around, playing Twenty Questions. It's a dangerous game ... I don't have to tell *you*. That sort of knowledge ...'

'Not *planned*,' I interrupted.

'You said ...'

'*Being* planned.'

'Is there a difference?' he asked.

'It's—it's ...' I struggled for the right words, then plumped for, 'Under consideration.'

'You sound like a blasted politician.'

'I'm serious,' I said.

'Don't think I'm *not*.' The narrowing of his eyes emphasised the truth of the remark. 'I find murder—even the murder of an animal like Paul Gunter—a very serious subject.'

'Oh, my God!' I breathed.

I'd made a complete balls of it. I'd wanted, so desperately to get Collins and Raff off the hook; to save them from their own stupidity. That ... and nothing more than that. I'd wanted to tell Sullivan—off the record—that two of our pals had taken leave of their senses. That they had to be stopped, before they smashed their own lives to hell and back. That's what I'd wanted—*all* I'd wanted ... a little assistance from the one man capable of giving it. And (God damn it!) what I had to say—the words I *had* to speak—wouldn't come out without choking me.

Sullivan let the silence ferment a little, then said, 'Well?'

I moved my shoulders. I still couldn't bring myself to say the words.

Sullivan growled, 'You have me, Charlie. All night, if necessary. I'm not leaving, till I know.'

'It's all your bloody fault,' I said, miserably.

'*My* fault?'

'That damn-fool speech you made at Collins's party. All that crappy talk about the Police not being a "vehicle for vengeance" ... some such bullshit. People thought you meant it.'

'I *did* mean it.'

'People took you seriously.'

'I *meant* them to take me seriously.'

'Too bloody seriously!' I grunted, heavily. 'You started something you're going to have to stop, Dick.'

'You mean ...' He gaped. 'Some silly bastard who was there, last night?'

I nodded, sadly.

'He's going to do Gunter? He's going to *murder* Paul Gunter?'

'You started it, mate.'

'For God's sake!'

'You planted the seed. Don't blame it if it grows.'

'Look—I didn't mean ...'

'You meant it.' I was suddenly very angry with this stupid A.C.C.(Crime). This gold-plated fuzz-boy who opened his mouth and said things he 'didn't mean'. I snapped, 'You meant it, Dick. You've just *said* you meant it.'

'At the time—at the time, I may have meant it ... but, bloody hell! After what had just happened. We all say things we think we mean—at the time ... till we've cooled down.'

'You're making excuses,' I accused him. 'You're crawling from under, mate. And you *can't*.'

He was nailed. The great Sullivan. The unbeatable—the incorruptible—Sullivan was licked. I'd said all the wrong things. I'd done all the wrong things. But, somehow, all the wrong things I'd said and done added up to the *right* thing. I'd dumped the baby—soiled nappy and all—right in Sullivan's lap, and he couldn't rid himself of it. For a moment, he'd tried. For a moment, he'd panicked. But not after my accusation. He was too complete a man. Too honest. Therefore, he accepted the accusation without rancour, stopped struggling, took a deep breath and blew out his cheeks in disgust.

'It has to be David Raff, of course,' he sighed. 'After last night, it has to be David.'

'David,' I confirmed, solemnly. 'Fixby's widow committed suicide. As I see it, that was the ...'

'Aye. I heard.' He looked miserable, and muttered, 'Bloody shocking.'

We had a moment or two of silence; a token requiem for a

copper and his wife, both killed by a bastard who couldn't be touched by the law.

'I suppose,' murmured Sullivan. 'It had to be David. He's still a little ... er—a little unpredictable.'

'And Collins?' I asked, gently.

'Henry Collins?' Sullivan looked puzzled.

'He's in it too.'

'*Collins?*' Disbelief dropped an expressive curtain across Sullivan's face.

I nodded.

'Jesus Christ!'

I said, 'And Collins hasn't had a nervous breakdown. He's not at all "unpredictable". And he's every bit as determined as Raff. So-o ... where do we go from here?'

'Anybody else?' asked Sullivan, quietly. Grimly.

'No. Just the two of them. Henry and David. They wanted me in ... but I wouldn't. That's how I know. That's why I'm so sure.'

'The hairbrained bloody idiots.'

'Aye—I know ... but what do we *do* about it?'

'If they murder Gunter, there's only one thing I *can* ...'

'*If* they murder him.'

'You say they've planned to ...'

'Not yet,' I interrupted. 'At the moment, they're just—er—talking about it. But not empty talk. They mean what they say. Up to this lunch time, they hadn't planned anything. They were still —er—discussing the means. Y'know ... *how* it might be possible. But they're serious, Dick. Believe me, it's not crank-talk. They'll reach a decision. Means and opportunity ... they'll work it out. Then they'll do it—or *try* to do it ... and then!'

'And then ...' Sullivan ended the sentence for me. 'Their feet won't touch. Not after what you've just told me.'

'Dick,' I pleaded, 'they're our friends.'

He nodded, slowly.

'They have to be stopped ... before it's too late.'

'How?'

'By you,' I said, bluntly. 'You tossed the idea into the air in the first place. They caught it. Okay—now you make 'em drop it.'

'It won't be easy.'

'Lean on 'em,' I growled. 'Shake 'em around a bit. If necessary, scare the hell out of 'em.'

'You've already reminded me,' he said, sourly. 'They're my friends.'

I let him have it, right in the teeth.

I said, 'Okay. Scare your friends—or arrest your friends ... that's your choice.'

He took a drink of the beer. A long, deep swallow. He placed the tankard on the carpet, alongside his chair, then struck a match and re-lighted his pipe. He took his time. He was (I knew) catching as thick a wedge of thinking space as possible. He had (I also knew) a lot to think about.

I gave him as much time as he wanted.

'I'll see Collins,' he said, at last. He spoke slowly. Thoughtfully. 'I'll warn him off. Meanwhile ...'

He gave me a long, hard look.

'Yes?' I asked.

He said, 'I want to know what's happening. Whether they've heeded the warning. I want *you* to be able to tell me.'

'How the hell ...'

'Get back with 'em,' he said, gruffly. 'Tell 'em you've changed your mind ... that you want in.'

'D'you think they'd believe me?' I asked, contemptuously.

'Why not?'

'After what I've told *you*?'

'Need they know?'

'How else would *you* know?' I asked.

'Kid 'em,' he growled. 'Lie to 'em. Lie well. Tell 'em you changed your mind, after you'd seen me ... tell 'em what a ring-tailed bastard I am, if that'll help.'

'Collins? You think Collins would fall for *that*?'

'I think he'd better.' He was suddenly all A.C.C.(Crime); he was all cop, and nothing else but cop, and a friend to no man. He said, 'I think you'd better make him fall for it, Charlie. I think you'd better lie, like you've never lied before, and make 'em believe you. They're already sailing close to the wind ... and you aren't too far behind. So *make* 'em believe you, Charlie. For everybody's sake.'

'Especially,' I sneered, 'for one honest and upright citizen called Paul Gunter.'

'You've been a copper,' said Sullivan, heavily. 'You're not just in from the backwoods. You know the rules of the game. Gunter's an innocent man, pending hard proof to the contrary. If he's murdered—if somebody attempts to murder him—the feathers'll fly ... and it's my job to make damn sure they fly!'

'Threats?' I asked, bitterly.

'No. Limitations.' He treated me to another of his quick, twisted smiles. He said, 'Look—don't think I'm ungrateful, Charlie. I know what telling me must have cost you. Now—do me a favour—consider what a word of warning might cost *me*. I give 'em the hard talk—I tell 'em to forget it—and they don't take good advice. What happens? They go ahead, and do Gunter. Great—I arrest 'em ... then what? I'm on ice, mate. It's not what they would do, it's what they *could* do. They could stand there, in the witness box, and say I *knew*. They could say I'd been warned ... that you'd warned me. And, by Christ, they'd be right! And that's me down the plug-hole ... because I didn't even try to stop 'em. So-o. Limitations, Charlie. Self-preservation. I want to know exactly how far they've gone, at any given moment. I want to know "when" and "how", with enough time to spare to let me build a brick wall between them and Gunter. Otherwise ...'

'Otherwise, we're all in the shit,' I said, bluntly.

Sullivan said, 'I couldn't have put it better.'

That night, I broke a rule. I took dope to make me sleep; Sodium Amytal—a couple of two-hundred-milligramme capsules. The doc had prescribed them ... 'For when you have trouble getting off. But be careful—they can become a habit.' I hated the damn things; false sleep wrapped up in little tubes of blue forgetfulness. I took one, maybe once a month, when the moods were blackest, and when nothing else could make me *not* remember what I was and

61

what I'd once been. On those nights, I would take one ... and hate myself for the weakness.

That night, I took two.

I dreamed.

I dreamed of her, and the hurtful thing was that she wasn't lonely. She was happy. And I should have been happy, because *she* was happy but, instead, her happiness made me want to cry out with pain. She had no right to be happy ... without me, she had no *right*! She had (or so the dream argued) taken my happiness, to add to her own. Stolen our combined happiness and left me only our combined misery. She wasn't lonely, she wasn't unhappy, she wasn't crippled ... and I was all those things, and more. And it wasn't fair. Damn it to hell, it wasn't fair! And (in my dream) I hated her, and reviled her, but she neither saw nor heard ... she was too busy being happy.

It was some sleep. Some dream.

I awoke with a mouth like a parrot's cage ... and told myself it was better than I deserved.

Sullivan replied, 'Come', to the knock on the door of his office. The door opened, Collins entered, Sullivan looked up from the foldered sheets he'd been checking, and said, 'Ah—Henry ... come in. Pull up a chair.'

Collins closed the door, positioned a high-backed chair across the desk from Sullivan, and sat down.

Sullivan glanced at the papers on the desk in front of him, smiled wry-mouthed, then said, 'Crime stats. For the chief's Annual Report. Something even you never had to wrestle with.'

Collins moved his shoulders, politely, and waited.

Sullivan closed the folder, leaned back in his chair, and said, 'I had a late night, last night, Henry.'

'Really?'

'Charlie Ripley sent for me. I was over at his place until the small hours.'

'Really?' repeated Collins.

'He sent for me,' said Sullivan, in a flat voice, 'in order to tell

me that you, and Raff, are planning to murder Paul Gunter. He's worried. Worried stupid. He thinks you're serious.'

'I am serious,' said Collins, quietly. 'So is Raff.'

Sullivan's hands were resting on the desk top. He closed the fingers into fists and shut his eyes.

With his eyes still shut, he breathed, 'God damn it, Henry! You can't do it. You're an intelligent man. You know bloody fine ... you can't do it.'

'Can ... and will,' said Collins, softly.

Sullivan opened his eyes, stared disbelief mixed with something not too far removed from hatred at the slim, ex-Hallsworth Hill superintendent, and rasped, 'I—I could stop it.'

'How?'

'I—I could ...'

'I'll make you a proposition, Richard.' For the first time since he'd entered Sullivan's office, Collins allowed himself a smile. It was a gentle smile, but with sadness at the mouth-corners. He said, 'Subject to David's approval, of course. Arrange for Paul Gunter to stand in a dock and plead "Guilty" to the murder of Detective Constable Fixby ... then we won't arrange the other thing.'

'How the merry Christ can I "arrange" ...'

'In that case—I'm sorry, Richard—Gunter has very little time left.'

After that night—after that dream—I needed to play truant from madness for a couple of hours. I sought sanity at Susan's place.

She and Chris lived in a neat little semi, on the outskirts of Sopworth.

Not that I'd ever been mad-keen about Sopworth (or, come to that, had either Susan or Chris); a valley townlet too far away from the fields and tops which made up much of Beachwood Brook Division to enjoy the fresh air of that division; a place of mills, light industry and a couple of brickworks. A small place—almost unknown, south of Doncaster—but with the doubtful boast that more millionaires owned various parts of it, size-for-size, than anywhere else in the U.K. ... but that none of the millionaires actually *lived* there.

Sopworth—but it had to be bobbied, and it needed a detective sergeant ... and Chris was *it*.

It was his Rest Day and, as the taxi braked in front of the gate, he straightened up from the mower with which he was trimming the few square yards of lawn.

He came to the taxi, gave me his arm as I eased myself onto the pavement, and said, 'Look—you've been told—ring ... don't go to the expense of a taxi, when you want to visit us. I'll come in the car for you.'

He meant it, too. It wasn't the normal, empty, son-in-law chat-up. We knew each other; as men, as fellow-cops, as colleagues in the everyday husband-and-wife battle for moral supremacy.

As we neared the door, he looked shamefaced, and said, 'I'll—er—y'know ... get back to the lawn, for a while.'

'Trouble?' I asked.

'Jesus!' He raised his eyes to the sky. 'Y'know, Charlie ... you sired a wildcat. She believes nothing. Nothing!'

'Do they ever?'

He spread his hands, helplessly, and returned to his grass.

As I opened the side door, Susan snapped, 'And don't think you can ...' She stopped, as she saw me, cried 'Pop!' and ran to fuss as I made heavier-weather than usual up the three shallow steps.

They were rowing ... much as normal, healthy married couples do row, occasionally. They were both so damn right but, at the same time, they were both so infernally wrong. They'd grow older. They'd grow out of it. Meanwhile, it was part of being in love.

I knew ... damn right I knew!

She settled me in a chair, made tea and sandwiches, then came to sit on the long-haired wool rug, with her back leaning against the arm of my chair.

'What about Chris?' I asked, innocently.

'What *about* Chris?'

'Doesn't *he* want a snack?'

'Look—pop ...'

'Kiss and make up,' I suggested, patiently.

'Has he been telling you ...'

'Nothing, sweetheart.'

'... a pack of lies?'

'Nothing, sweetheart,' I repeated. 'Just that he's scared to come inside ... that's all.'

'I'll—I'll kill him,' she exaggerated. 'So help me, I'll kill him.'

'But not today ... eh?' I chuckled.

She looked up at me, with all the innocent concern in the world, and said, 'Pop, can I ask you a question?'

'Go ahead,' I encouraged.

'A very serious question.'

'Uhu.'

'A very—y'know ... a very *personal* question?'

'As personal as you want to make it, sweetheart.'

'And you'll give me an honest answer?'

'As honest as I know how,' I promised.

She moistened her lips, flared her nostrils a little, took a deep breath, then said, 'Okay ... what the hell is there about a woman's tits that interest men?'

I claim credit. I did not slosh tea all down the front of my trousers. Not only that, but I kept a very deadpan expression fixed firmly to my face. And that (take it from me) needed a double-helping of sheer will-power.

I looked down at her and, very solemnly, said, 'Women's tits, I suppose.'

'Eh?'

'That's what—er—interests 'em ... since you ask.' I paused, then added, 'By the way, *why* do you ask?'

'That animal,' she flared. 'That snake-in-the-grass I married.'

'Is he—er ... "interested"?' I asked, innocently.

'I'll say. Last night, at Sopworth Section Dance ...'

'... I didn't know. I've lost track of the dance dates, since ...'

'... there was this *female*.'

'... I left the force.'

'Y'know ... blowsy. An absolute *cow*. Y'know the sort I mean?'

'I know exactly what you mean, sweetheart.'

'Top-heavy. God! ... she was *deformed*.'

65

'As bad as that?'

As bad as *that*, she insisted. 'And he danced with her, five times. *Five times!*'

'That's a lot of dances,' I agreed.

'And always up close. Y'know ... holding her tight against his chest. God! ... it's a wonder *she* didn't end the night flat-chested.'

'Is that what the row's about?' I asked.

'That ... and that he swears he doesn't even *know* her.'

'And does he?' I asked.

'I don't know.' The female fury was suddenly turned off, as with a tap, and she was suddenly very miserable—but 'happy' miserable, if you know what I mean ... and, if you don't, you have no soul, so who cares? She moved her head and stared, wide-eyed and lost, at the wool rug, and murmured, 'I don't know, pop. I don't think so ... but I don't *know*.'

'He says he doesn't,' I reminded her, gently.

'Yes, but ...' She sighed.

'Of course, if he's a liar ...'

'Who says he's a liar?' The mood switched, again. This time, from sorrow to outrage. 'Look—whatever else he is, he isn't a ...'

'So-o,' I said, solemnly, 'we're back to square one. Big tits.'

'Whatever else, they weren't *square*.' She giggled, and it was like the rays of a sun slanting out from behind a thundercloud.

'We're men,' I said softly. And this time, I meant it. 'We're weak. That's why we marry, sweetheart. To give us what we haven't got ... strength.'

'Pop. You were never weak.' Something not too far short of hero-worship was there, in the voice and in the eyes, and I wished to God I deserved some of it. 'You're just about the strongest man I've ever known ... and the most decent.'

'You could be hopelessly biased, sweetheart.'

'You're a nice man. A very ...'

'And Chris.'

'He's—he's ...' She gave a tiny shrug, as if to shake off the last of the marital spat. 'He's okay ... I suppose.'

'By this time,' I said, pointedly 'that lawn should be well and truly cut. And he'll be ready for a snack.'

'I suppose.' She pushed herself to her feet, and murmured, 'I suppose that's what I'm here for ... to feed the brute.'

A nice couple. Perfectly matched. Oh, they'll have their rows—they'll bawl each other out, periodically ... but that's part of it. Part of married life; a part they'll gradually grow out of, as they each accept the other, warts and all, and stop asking for perfection. It's what makes the early years exciting, and the middle years beautiful. It's what the word 'love' means. A word that, if the truth be told, is not too far from 'hate'—because one is not the opposite of the other ... the opposite of 'love' is 'indifference'. Not in the dictionary, maybe. But in life.

I would like to tell them—Susan and Chris—I would like to explain something to them which, in their presence, I could never bring myself to say.

That they are like Elaine and myself, in many ways; like *we* were, when we were their age. And they make the same mistakes and, with luck, they will learn from those mistakes. That (for example) they have each placed the other on a pedestal and that, when either one exhibits some human failing—some tiny, personal foible—which is not in keeping with pedestal-squatting, the other becomes enraged. Disappointed. Hurt. And that (and *only* that) is what triggers off the rows. That nobody—not even Susan, not even Chris—is perfect. But that the imperfections make them unique, and priceless. That the imperfections are what brought them together, and made them close.

Christ, if I could only put it better! If I could only tell them in language which sounds a little less like the cliché-heavy mouthings of the sob-sisters. That they are *Chris* and *Susan*, and that that is sufficient; that that is the source of the magic from which stems every moment of their happiness ... and from which will stem every second of their misery.

Look beyond the words.

See what I'm trying to say.

Please! ... *understand me.*

* * *

I stayed for quick lunch, then away. They wanted me to make a day of it, but I'd more sense; it was Chris's Rest Day, they'd patched up a stupid quarrel, and now they had the privacy of a bedroom and the comfort of a double-bed ... the last thing they needed was a clapped-out old has-been, hanging around and preventing nature from taking its course.

For this reason, too, I insisted upon taking a taxi back to the bungalow. Chris had better, and more important, things to do than drive me around.

The Peugeot was parked less than a hundred yards away, and across the road, from the bungalow. Too far away to see who was in it ... as if I couldn't guess. Too far away to read the registration plates ... as if I needed to do that.

I didn't know anybody who ran a Peugeot. They're great cars ... but a little pricey. My friends and acquaintances concentrated upon less expensive chariots.

However ...

The taxi drove off, and I waited.

Less than five minutes later somebody thumbed the front door bell-push and I called, 'Don't stand in a draught, Gunter. Come inside.'

It was a guess—but a good guess ... the Peugeot was parked by the gate.

He strolled into the main room of the bungalow. Big, dark-skinned, dark-haired, immaculately clothed and as sure of himself as the eastern skyline is as sure of tomorrow's sunrise.

'You knew,' he murmured.

'I can read tea leaves,' I threw back at him.

His mouth curved, and he chuckled; a silent, closed-mouth chuckle which moved his shoulders slightly.

He sat down, eased the material from one of his knees, and crossed his legs. Relaxed. At ease. Already (apparently!) in complete charge of the situation.

'Please make yourself comfortable,' I said, sarcastically.

'Of course.' The voice went with the man; deep, resonate ...

the brand of voice which goes with world-class operatic baritones. He said, '*The Silver Bowl* ... not the best place for a conspiracy.'

'Not with your boys listening,' I agreed.

'Whose choice?' he asked.

'Collins ... I think.'

'Collins?' Once more there was the silent chuckle. 'That man should come out of the clouds. I don't only control brothels.'

I grunted some sort of reply, and left the way open for him to do some more talking.

'Can they do it?' he asked.

'Somebody,' I said, grimly, 'shot John Kennedy. And even *you* aren't as well-protected as that.'

'Will they try?'

'Ask Collins,' I suggested. 'Ask Raff. They'll give you a better answer than I can.'

'The crazy man,' mused Gunter. 'He'd try. He's crazy enough to try *anything*.'

'Not crazy,' I growled.

'No?' He seemed mildly surprised.

'He hates your guts. That doesn't make him crazy. That makes him normal.'

He slipped a hand under his jacket, and took out a cigar-case from the inside pocket. He opened the case, and held it, offered, towards me. I took a cigar—and why not? ... they were good cigars, and he wasn't stupid enough to think he could buy anything with rolled tobacco-leaf.

He chose a cigar, returned the case to his inside pocket, took out a cigar-cutter, snipped the end of his cigar and, as he did these things, he talked.

He said, 'You interest me, Ripley. The only cop who's ever slung me over the wall ... that makes you special. I should hate you, but I don't. You were a uniformed bull, but you were a man. Not weak—like Raff ... you didn't crack when the pressure was on. Not like Collins—effeminate ... too damn highbrow to know what it's like to bleed. You were a bastard, Ripley. And I admire bastards.'

He tossed the cigar-cutter towards me and, as I caught it, I said, 'That makes you love yourself more than any other man I know.'

The silent chuckle came again.

He gripped the cigar between his teeth, felt in his pocket for a lighter, and said, 'You were the odd man out, at *The Silver Bowl*.'

'Uhu.' I used the cutter on the cigar with care.

'Why?'

'You wouldn't understand,' I growled. 'Not even with diagrams.'

'You don't go for murder ... that it?'

'Something along those lines.' I finished with the cutter and threw it back to him.

He caught it, slipped it into his pocket, leaned forward and flicked the lighter into flame as he said, 'I don't buy that one, Ripley. Not raw.'

'I've already said.' I rolled the end of the cigar in the lighter's flame, and inhaled top-class nicotine fumes. 'You don't understand the language.'

'You've killed.' He leaned back and lighted his own cigar, talking between the puffs. 'I've followed your career, Ripley. You're no pansy. You've killed—been instrumental in killing ... so, why not go along with Collins and Raff.'

'Not murder,' I said. 'That stinks a little ... even to a pig.'

'We die,' he said, gently. He dropped the lighter back into its pocket. 'We all die, one day. Some sooner, some later ... that's all.'

Very deliberately, I said, 'Aye—*sooner* ... if you happen to be called Fixby.'

'He asked for it,' he said, calmly.

'And you?'

'There are options. Always.' That voice—that magnificent voice—carried this man's absolute belief. 'You go under, or you walk on the other guy. That, or you step aside. Fixby wouldn't step aside, and I wouldn't go under. What else was left?'

'His wife?' I suggested, meaningly. 'She was left ... a widow.'

'Don't play with words, Ripley.' Soft warning was in his tone. 'I am not here because I like the company.'

'Unless you dropped the latch,' I growled, 'the door is still unlocked.'

'And if I do?' His eyes mocked me through a gathering haze of cigar smoke. 'If I walk out of here. Will that bring Fixby back to life? Will that mean his wife hasn't buckled, and followed him?'

'You know? ... about her?' I murmured.

'In that town ... *everything.*'

'Aye—you would—your narks at *The Silver Bowl* no doubt ...'

'Before you knew,' he interrupted, softly. 'Before Collins knew. Yeah—before even *Raff* knew ... before his wife had time to go back and tell him.'

'You felt proud, I hope,' I said, contemptuously.

'I felt nothing. Why the hell should I? The choice was hers. Options ... remember?'

I realised something. Something which (come to think about it) I'd known for years. That Paul Gunter was as near to a 'one off' as any human being is ever likely to be. It wasn't that he was consciously bad, or consciously evil. He was Paul Gunter ... period. What he was, and what he always had been. What he always would be. A mutation, if you like. A non-human, without feelings and without human failings. He did things, because he wanted to do them and that, of itself, was a good enough reason. He'd used the cigar-cutter because, without its use, he would not have been able to enjoy the cigar and, for the same reason (and with as little thought) he would commit murder, or drive decent men and women to suicide ... in order that he, himself, might enjoy the luxuries of life.

I decided to do more than merely talk to him. I decided to *converse* with him; to ask questions and explore his answers in the hope that I might see what made such a man tick.

I started with the biggest question of all.

I said, 'Okay—let's assume, for the sake of argument, that you murdered Fixby and made life unbearable for his wife ... why not kill Collins and Raff? Why not kill *them*, before they can kill *you*?

'Because I, too, have options.'

'Agreed.'

'I opt not to take unnecessary risks.'

'You mean after the evening before last?' I said. 'After what happened in *The Woodchopper's Arms*?'

'That?' His lip curled, ever so slightly.

'You lived dangerously, for a few minutes,' I said.

He drew on the cigar, and shook his head, slowly.

He said, 'You people—the cops—you don't even understand yourselves. One copper. Two ... three, at the most. It might have been dangerous. But, how many were in there? Half a hundred?'

'About,' I agreed.

'And their women. Say a hundred ... round figures. They're all going to sit back, and say nothing? They're *all* going to commit perjury? Oh, no—I was safe, Ripley ... too many cops. Not one of them could trust *all* the others.'

'Raff nearly pulled it,' I teased.

'You know better,' he mocked.

'Do I?'

'You said as much—the truth—in *The Silver Bowl*.'

'Word for word?' I murmured.

He shrugged, and the shrug was my answer.

'Okay,' I said. 'So, if it was delivered, word for word, you know they mean it.'

'Did I say not?' he countered.

'So, why not kill *them*?'

'There are ...' He paused to enjoy another draw on his cigar. 'There are risks which can be eliminated. Take Fixby—as you say, let's assume, for the sake or argument, that I had something to do with his removal—Fixby was a nothing. Bu-ut ... even a nothing can create problems. Other men live. Men who have knowledge. Men I can trust ... but I trust no man, completely. They are a risk—a carefully calculated risk—and they continue to be a risk.'

'Eliminate the—er—risk,' I suggested.

'And create more risks?' He shook his head in mock-sadness.

'It's a spiral staircase,' I said.

'Something like that.'

'One day, you'll fall off.'

'No. Not if I test each step, before I trust my weight to it. Not if I have a firm handrail. I've a good head for heights, Ripley ... I won't fall off.'

He pushed himself up from the chair and strolled to the side-

board. The ash-trays were on the sideboard; twin, onyx ash-trays
... a wedding present from one of Elaine's uncles. Gunter brought
the ash-trays across the room, placed one on the coffee-table
alongside my chair and took its partner and placed it on the
carpet by the side of his own chair. He settled himself in the
chair, again. He leaned sideways and eased a good half-inch of
pale grey ash from the end of his cigar and into the concave of the
onyx.

He drew deeply on the cigar, before he spoke again.

He said, 'We've already played around with one assumption,
Ripley—that I had something to do with Fixby's death—now,
let's play around with another. Let's assume Collins and Raff are
serious. That they do intend to murder me.'

'That's a good assumption,' I said. 'A very safe assumption.'

'Okay.' He moved his head in a single nod. 'And, if they try,
and succeed, I'm dead ... that's one option. But, if they try, and ...
fail—that's another option ... what then?'

'It's a gamble I wouldn't like to take,' I growled.

'What then?' he repeated.

'If they fail?'

'What then?' he asked for the third time.

'Attempted Murder,' I said.

'Ah! ... and?'

'Do I have to tell you?'

'I would,' he said, 'like verification. From the horse's mouth.'

'Prison,' I said, flatly.

'A long stretch ... wouldn't you say?'

I nodded.

'So-o ...' He enjoyed one of his silent, tight-lipped chuckles.
'All I need do is make sure they fail. Their own kind will take
care of the rest.'

(Looking back—as I tell this—there is still an air of unreality
about that conversation with Gunter. There is a fairy-tale quality
... but a fairy-tale, strictly from the warped minds of the Brothers
Grimm. We talked about 'options' and 'spiral staircases' and

'handrails'. What we *really* talked about was graft, corruption and murder. Gunter knew it, and I knew it, and there was no reason on God's earth why we shouldn't have called a shithouse a shithouse, and have done with it. But, instead, we were calling it 'The Powder Room'—or some such crap . . . and we were kidding ourselves that it smelled the sweeter for another name.

Correction—*I* was kidding myself . . . I doubt if Gunter ever kidded himself in his whole life!

I think that was the strength of the man. One of his strengths . . . one of his many strengths. That he was, by far, the most honest man I'd ever met. Whatever else he was—however rotten he was—self-honesty was the one thing he had in abundance. As far as Gunter was concerned, there was nothing incongruous about sitting, relaxed, in the armchairs—enjoying expensive cigars—and, almost casually, discussing the pros and cons of murder.

Installing a shower is part of a plumber's craft.

Murder was part of Gunter's craft.

And that—I swear!—is how normal, and everyday, the conversation was.)

'We are,' I said, tauntingly, 'making another "assumption".'

'Is that a fact?' he asked, with interest.

'That they'll miss,' I explained.

He eyed me a question.

'Attempted Murder,' I amplified. 'If it's only that, you're still alive. But, if it's more than that, all your—er—options come to a sudden stop.'

'I'm dead?' he murmured.

'As the Flat Earth Theory,' I agreed.

He smiled. It was not his previous silent chuckle, this time. This time it was a smile—a genuine curve of the lips . . . but not a nice smile, and a very loaded smile.

He enjoyed some cigar smoke, then said, 'You know a lot about death, Ripley . . . agreed?'

'I've handled a few murder enquiries. I've . . .'

'No. I mean death.'

For the first time, the direction of the conversation eluded me. I grunted, 'I've seen a few corpses, if that's what you mean. I've ...'

'Personal experience,' he said, softly.

I snarled, 'If you mean my wife, you can keep your foul-mouthed ...'

'*Personal*,' he interrupted, slowly.

'Spit it out, Gunter,' I said, harshly. 'If you have something to say, say it. In real words.'

'Okay.' He drew on the cigar, nodded once towards my legs, then said, 'From the belly-button, down. You're dead. I'd call that a very personal experience of death ... as near as it's possible to get, short of the real thing. Okay?'

'If it's any business of yours,' I agreed, coldly.

'Oh, I'm making it my business.'

'Don't bother. I don't need ...'

'It's another of my options.'

'Eh?' I stared at him.

'There is,' he said, 'a certain Swiss surgeon. I've asked around. I know what I'm talking about, Ripley. Check, if you must ... but you needn't. He could get you walking—without irons ... maybe. I'm told it's a fifty-fifty chance. Maybe a sixty-forty. But a chance. If it's possible—and it could *be* possible—it means an expensive operation, and a long stay in a Swiss clinic. An expensive clinic. I'm told this guy can work near-miracles ... if the bread comes heavy enough.'

He paused, and watched my face.

'So?' I breathed.

'You *want* to walk?' he asked, softly.

'Let's say I want to walk,' I whispered.

'It's on the house.'

'It's ... It's ...'

'On the house,' he repeated. And that voice—that tone—made the offer almost boringly mundane. A bagatelle. A throw-away gesture. A crumb, tossed to a starving beggar by a passer-by who, for the moment, is feeling big-hearted. That's how unimportant he made the offer sound. He said, 'All expenses ... everything. If it works ... okay. If not, ten grand for the inconvenience it might have caused.'

It was one hell of a proposition.

He was offering me renewed life—he was offering to make me whole, again ... and (damn him!) he knew it. A fifty-fifty chance? A sixty-forty chance? Christ ... the quacks had once said I'd never again stand upright!

Of course I couldn't refuse the offer. I *couldn't*. It was the one offer—the one corruption—I could not draw my hand away from.

He waited, and he knew what the answer must be.

I drew on the cigar, to steady my nerves—to give my voice time enough to handle the shake which, I knew, would have been there with an immediate agreement—then, when I spoke, I tried to make my words sound as calmly off-handed as his own.

I said, 'For what?'

'Ripley—you're not *that* stupid.'

'You've already used an expression. Let's use it again. "From the horse's mouth".'

'I would,' he said, carefully, 'prefer it to be *Attempted* Murder.'

'I can't stop them,' I said sombrely.

'I don't want you to stop them ... not from *trying*.'

'And, if they succeed.'

'They won't.'

'You sound very sure, Gunter.'

'Three question,' he murmured. 'How? When? Where? With the answers to those three questions, I'll stop them. I'll let them try—I'll let them get so far—*then* ...'

He leaned sideways to ease another good half-inch of ash from his cigar, and into the ash-tray. A simple movement—an innocent movement—but he made it look remarkably like a decapitation.

'No counter-killing,' I said, with a rush.

'Why should I?' He seemed surprised at my remark.

'You could,' I argued.

'Indeed.' He nodded ... we were, by this time, calling shit-houses shithouses.

'I've no guarantee.'

'Logic,' he smiled. 'We've already covered the ground. It would create "risks".'

'Okay.' I nodded. Satisfied. 'No-counter-killings.'

In a pseudo-patient voice, he said, 'Ripley, I want them removed ... that's all. Not, necessarily dead. Merely somewhere where they can do me no harm. Prison ... that suits my purpose, equally as well as a grave.' He gave his quick, silent chuckle, then added, 'It *is* the grave, as far as they're concerned. They'll die in prison. The crazy man, for sure. Collins ... the chances are good.'

'Fifty-fifty?' I asked, bitterly.

'He won't be ordering casserole of partridge ... that, for sure.'

(I was under no disillusion, you understand. I was now 'Gunter's man'. I'd said 'Yes' ... not in that single, short and specific word, but in everything else. I had not said 'No'. I had not said 'Perhaps'. I knew damn well what I'd said, by implication if not by mouth, and so did Paul Gunter.

He'd dangled the juiciest carrot ever thought up, and I'd grabbed.

At the moment, I was taking the strain.

All I needed to know, now, was the weight of the cart I had to pull.)

'Get back in with Collins and the crazy man,' said Gunter.

'That won't be easy,' I protested.

'Tonight.'

'Look—how the hell can I ...'

'Tonight,' repeated Gunter. 'I want to know fast. There's a table booked, in your name, at *The Silver Bowl*. A table for three. Use it ... and get back with them.'

It wasn't a 'conversation' any more. We were no longer equals. It was now master and servant and, in the less-than-subtle change of tone and choice of words, Gunter made that very plain. He wasn't merely talking. He was now giving orders.

'Look,' I said, 'they're not dumb ... especially Collins. They may not believe me.'

'Make them believe you.'

'How the hell can I ...'

'That problem is all yours, Ripley. Solve it your own way ... just solve it. Just convince them. You're a copper—you talk their language ... use it.'

'I'll try,' I said, heavily.

'You'll do a damn sight better than *try*.' He stood up from the chair, and walked towards the door. He said, 'The dinner is booked for eight. I'll have a report—verbatim—before midnight. Work hard, Ripley ... keep remembering Switzerland.' He took a packed wallet from his hip pocket, fingered out three ten-pound notes, dropped them onto the seat of the chair, near the door, and said, 'Expenses. Eat well. Drink some good wine. And lie convincingly.'

He opened the door and began to walk from the room. The timing was perfect. With the door starting to close behind him, he turned, looked at me with hard, expressionless eyes, and gave me the final 'or else'.

He said, 'Oh—and Ripley—be advised. Don't get clever. I'll know *that*, too. You have a daughter, I think. Word says you're pretty close. When you're not concentrating on Switzerland, concentrate on her. Anything slightly off-key, and I promise ... you'll *both* need leg-irons.'

He closed the door.

Less than two minutes later I heard the Peugeot start up, and drive away.

You know what?

Other men can go for a walk. They can stroll around while they wait for their minds to play magician with the coloured silks of thought. They have certain choices. They can stride, or meander—wander, aimlessly, or even run—while the God-given computer between their ears buzzes and clicks, and gets all the numerals into good order before it comes up with the right answer.

I know. I used to be such a man and, in those days, too, I had

78

my quota of problems. Agreed, they were problems about law-enforcement—problems about shortage of manpower—problems about lack of evidence—but, however great, they could always be *walked* out. There is a link between physical activity and mental activity. I can't prove it ... I just know! I have done it too often, and with too much success, ever to doubt it. I have walked miles ... thinking. And always, at the end of the walk, the solution has been so bloody obvious.

At the *end* of the walk.

Other men can go for a walk ... but I couldn't!

What I could do, I did. I hobbled out of the bungalow, stood (propped on elbow crutches) in the front garden, breathed good air and tried to put the right nut on the right bolt. Jesus, how I tried! I rammed those thoughts through my skull at such speed, I damn near caused friction. I damn near set my brain alight.

And the end product?

I will explain it, in detail ... poverty-stricken though it may be.

Item.

Nobody (other than Collins and Raff) wanted Collins and Raff to murder Paul Gunter.

Gunter's objection sprang from a natural, and understandable, desire for happy, and prosperous, longevity.

Sullivan's objection was based upon his professional integrity; that he was A.C.C.(Crime) in the police area where the killing was most likely to take place; that (thanks to my big mouth) the crime wouldn't even need detecting ... Sullivan would know, immediately, who to arrest.

My objection was similar to that of Sullivan's. I didn't give a damn about Gunter, but I gave considerably more than a damn about my friends, and the last thing I wanted was to see Collins and Raff stand in a dock, charged with a killing.

On a simple count of heads, therefore, the scheme was out-voted, three-to-two. A spanner was needed in the mechanism and

79

(as I saw it) I was the only person capable of ramming that spanner between the cogs.

Item.
Gunter already knew about the Collins/Raff lunacy. *The Silver Bowl* was not the safe place everybody thought it was; it was one of Gunter's many listening posts, around the city.

What was said in that restaurant would reach the ears of Paul Gunter, Esq., and this might (or might not) be used to advantage. Whether, or not, to let Collins and Raff into this little secret was something I had yet to decide. Friendship suggested I should tell them. Common gumption suggested I *shouldn't* ... otherwise they might change eating-houses and kybosh any advantage to be gained by this secret knowledge.

Item.
Sullivan also knew about the Collins/Raff lunacy ... and, if Sullivan had done the favour I'd asked of him, Collins and Raff *knew* that Sullivan knew.

More than that. Even supposing Sullivan hadn't mentioned my name, Collins and Raff would know that *I* was the informer; that I was the louse (in their eyes) who'd gone running to the authorities, and narked.

It was a fair assumption. If you plan to stop somebody's breath, you don't advertise the fact in a national newspaper. You keep the information limited to a very close circle of intimate friends. And, if the fuzz suddenly know as much as *you* know, the source of their information doesn't take too much tracing.

Ergo ...

Item.
Collins and Raff knew I'd already turned stool-pigeon.

That my reasons were personal—that they were prompted by genuine concern and friendship—didn't matter. As of now, Collins and Raff didn't trust me. I was suspect. I was more than suspect. I was a treacherous bastard.

Nevertheless ...

Item.

I had to worm my way back into the conspiracy. Somehow, I had to back-track to the starting-gate and turn the present duo into the previously contemplated trio. I had to *make* Collins and Raff trust me once more. I had to 'prove' that I'd had second thoughts; that I'd changed my mind; that (despite everything, and despite telling Sullivan of the scheme) I wanted Gunter dead. That I wanted a hand in this murder. That there was nothing—nothing!—they couldn't tell me, and that I wouldn't keep to myself.

Because ...

Item.

What the hell it cost—what the *hell* it cost!—Susan was not going to be made a cripple. It mattered not how many lies I had to tell—how much treachery I had to commit—who lived, or who died, who went to prison, or who did not go to prison—anything! ... but *Susan was not going to be made a cripple.*

And Gunter could do it. Whether he would do it—whether he'd risk making me his enemy and, as such, unleashing the hounds of the whole Police Service at his throat in my search for revenge, wasn't important ... that he was capable of it was enough. And he was capable of it. And, more than that—worse than that—I knew Gunter well enough to know that he didn't bluff. He didn't threaten, unless he was willing (and able) to carry out that threat.

Gunter could do it.

Gunter *would* do it.

But, if that's what he wanted—if that's what he asked—I'd

81

crawl on my belly and kiss his feet, rather than let it happen.
And ...

Item.

I wanted to walk again.

Does that sound mean? Selfish? Petty? Does that sound dishonourable? Or is that old-fashioned virtue, honour something, these days, strictly for the birds? Was it lowered, with the Union Jack, when we wiped the pink parts off the map of the world and stared sneering at Kipling's verse?

I wouldn't know. I'm still enough of a square to think that honour is a vital part of every complete man; that a man contemptuous of honour is, by simple definition, a man to be mistrusted.

And yet (God help me!) I wanted to walk again.

All right ... *all right!* ...

You are whole human beings; complete men, who take their completeness for granted. You are not old. You are not infirm. You are (to use the words of Elaine) 'in your middle years'. With the wisdom of life behind you, but still young enough to take advantage of that wisdom. The word 'prime' is often used, and that word is another way of saying 'perfection'; the perfect age, when experience has been learned and vitality is not yet lost.

Now think of me, at that moment of decision.

I, too, was of that age group. I, too, could still have lived a full life; could still have been active; could still have loved, and expressed my love, had the memory of Elaine ever allowed me to do so.

But I couldn't. I could do none of these things.

Because I couldn't even do that which a three-year-old can do. I couldn't even *walk!*

This is an honest narrative. As honest, and as subjective, as I can make it. The truth is, therefore, that Gunter had offered me a salvation. Many salvations. The salvation of, once more, being a complete man. The salvation of simple ablution, without bars and pulleys. The salvation of the ordinary use of a lavatory, without indignity bordering upon debasement. All these salvations, stemming from that one, monumental salvation of, once again, being able to walk.

No man will ever know the power—the gut-tearing sorrow—of the five words which capsulated the one argument which (Gunter knew) could turn me into a Judas ... *I WANTED TO WALK AGAIN*.

The end-product of my considerations, standing in the front garden of the bungalow. Pathetic?—agreed ... but a foundation upon which I had to build some sort of structure of activity.

I hobbled into the cottage, and telephoned Collins. Fortunately, he was at home, fortunately, he was free that evening and he'd be delighted to be my guest at a reciprocal meal at *The Silver Bowl*. Yes—he was quite sure David hadn't anything planned for the evening ... David usually stayed at home, watching T.V. in the evenings. He'd check, of course ... but I could, more or less, count on it.

Why didn't I come over to his place for a couple of hours, before we both went on to *The Silver Bowl*? A chat and a drink? And he had some new records and tapes he thought I'd be interested in.

I agreed.

And why not? ... the betrayal had to start somewhere.

Taxis. That's another thing. Taxis don't come cheap. I was spending a small fortune on taxis and, contrary to popular myth, a copper's pension (even the pension of an ex-chief superintendent) doesn't cover the cost of a luxury life-style.

I phoned for a taxi and, by the time it arrived at the bungalow,

I was ready for the first move in my act of disgrace.

Collins's place was nice. It was a ground-floor flat in one of the residential parts of the city; towards the end of a tree-lined cul-de-sac, away from the noise and the bustle.

Externally, the building looked mildly monstrous; a pile of solidly built Victoriana, tasteless enough to make even Sir John Betjeman clap a hand to his forehead in horror. It personified (or so I suspected) the man who had designed it and the man who had originally built and lived in it ... pompous and Presbyterian —self-made, stiff-necked and arrogant—a humourless, mid-nineteenth-century by-product who was a martinet to his wife, a lord and master to his family, a model of pseudo-respectability to his tight circle of carefully chosen friends, and a source of steady income to the whores of the town.

Externally, it made you want to puke. Internally (as far as Collins's flat was concerned) it was all diffident and restrained elegance.

The main room was large enough, and high enough, to allow the near-antique furniture to look genuinely functional. It was there to be used and, in its use, to give pleasure above and beyond the beauty of its lines. The high-backed wing-chairs—a matching pair—studded and upholstered in ox-blood leather; built by some chair-maker with a yearning for immortality via his craft; heavy and embracing, and made to give comfort throughout a dozen lifetimes. A brass-bound 'military chest' doing excellent service as a coffee-table; the polished metal playing perfect visual counterpoint to the dull sheen of the beeswaxed surface of seasoned oak; positioned between the wing-chairs and (unlike most conventional coffee-tables) utterly imperious to the accidental knock by a clumsy foot, or leg. A settle; a beautiful thing of slender line and green baize; of a delicacy which masked the subtle strength which had been built into its design; with tiny inlays whose minute detail only became apparent when searched for.

These were some of the pieces which made up the furniture in the main room of Collins's flat. They were a measure of the man himself. They were part of him. They reflected his personality, perfectly.

As did the few pictures which graced the walls.

Two Dürers—the small positioned above, and slightly to one side of, the large ... each, in its own way, showing the immaculate eye for detail enjoyed by Albrecht Dürer.

Until I'd met, and grown to know, Collins, I'd known little about art. *The Stag At Bay* had been my idea of a pretty good painting. Collins had educated me. Not deliberately—not condescendingly—but by allowing me to see genuine art, and passing comment as if I, too, could see what he could see. Thus he had *made* me see, and thus he had widened my appreciation and enriched my life.

And, of all the masterpieces, those two Dürers always, to me, meant 'Collins'.

They were not, of course, originals ... but they were both magnificent copies.

A Hare. The smaller of the two. Photographic in its every tiny detail. The ears, the whiskers, the eyes, the nose, the claws ... everything meticulously—almost three-dimensionally—accurate. It was as if God had asked Dürer to design for Him a hare and, from that masterpiece of a design, every other hare in creation had been copied. If you watched that picture long enough, there was an optical illusion. It happened, every time. The nostrils seemed to quiver, slightly and the eyes took on the hint of sudden alarm. The impression was that the timid creature was going to take fright, and lope from the framed surround.

That was *A Hare* and, when you saw it, you were quite sure that nobody—not even Albrecht Dürer—could create a likeness with more absolute detail.

Then you lowered your eyes, and saw the larger of the two Dürers, and realised that he could and, indeed, *had*.

Study of Plants. Not as well known, perhaps as his *Study of Hands in Adoration*—not as immediately breath-catching as the *Study of the Head of an Old Man*—but, for my money, a single reason for Albrecht Dürer having walked this earth and, in itself, a more than sufficient reason.

Once (before I'd seen Collins's copy) the wife of a close friend—

a young woman who knew more about art and beauty than I'll ever know—tried to describe Dürer's *Study of Plants* to me ... but without a copy with which to demonstrate. She explained that the picture gave an impression; that Dürer seemed to have taken a patch of tiny, uncultivated wilderness and dropped a bottomless cake-tin over it; that (or so it seemed) he'd drawn a circle around the edge of the cake-tin, lifted the cake-tin and directed every last ounce of his powers of concentration upon the miniature world encircled by his own self-imposed boundary.

The result was his *Study of Plants*. Grasses, leaves, weeds, fungi, miniaturised foliage ... a whole Lilliputian world of botanical perfection which Dürer had discovered, lifted in the palm of his hand, and presented to mankind.

Those two pictures—*A Hare* and *Study of Plants*—are, to me everything that Henry Collins ever was, or ever will be. Uncomplicated but, at the same time, exceptional. Magnificent but, again at the same time, worldly and everyday.

'You still like them, Charles?'

I stopped staring at the Dürers, worked to twist myself round, and said, 'As much as ever. One day, that damn hare is going to spot all that grass, jump down and start nibbling. And, when it does, I want to see it.'

Collins smiled, waved a hand towards one of the wing-chairs, and said, 'An aperitif, I thought. Before we go on to the meal. Medium-dry sherry ... all right?'

'Fine. Fine.'

I worked my way to the wing-chair and lowered myself into what might laughingly be called a 'sitting position'. The glasses of sherry were waiting on the military-chest coffee-table. There was also a large, crystal ash-tray, a silver table-lighter and an inlaid, sandalwood-and-ivory cigarette box.

'All mod cons' for the elegant bachelor who already has everything ... and, having given birth to the thought, my mind was immediately ashamed of its own petty envy.

Collins sat in the second wing-chair, and we tasted the sherry.

'Do you approve?' smiled Collins.

I said, 'Nice ... very nice.'

'Good.' He moved his head towards the cigarette-box. 'Help yourself, Charles. Or, if you prefer your pipe ...'

'No—no, thanks. I—er—I don't feel like a smoke. Not at the moment.'

For a few minutes, we sipped at the sherry. They were awkward minutes—friendly, but awkward—because each of us was waiting for the other to say the first words.

I out-waited Collins.

He murmured, 'Richard asked me to call in at his office.'

'Sullivan?' It was a damn-fool question—of course he meant Sullivan—but I wanted him to say more.

He said, 'I take it, Charles, that your intentions were good. I don't ask. I take that for granted ...'

'Thanks.'

'... but that does not make it any less—shall we say?—*sneaky*.'

'Mistaken,' I corrected him, gruffly.

'David doesn't know.'

'Thanks for that, too,' I said.

'David ...' He paused, as if seeking the precise terminology. Then, he murmured, 'David has enough problems. Too many. Sometimes they tend to overburden him.'

I loved that word. '*Overburden.*' It was pure 'Henry Collins'; it said everything, but without being hurtful.

I leaned the back of my head against the leather of the wing-chair, looked up at the high ceiling, and said, 'And I was wrong, too.'

'To tell Richard?'

'To tell him—aye ... but not to come in with you, in the first place.'

'Really?' He sounded politely surprised.

'It's too late now, of course,' I said, to the ceiling.

'It—er—it doesn't follow,' he said, slowly.

I bent my head, and looked across the military chest and into his face. I hoped to hell I could lie a lot better than I could walk.

I said, 'In your shoes ...' then stopped.

'Yes?' he encouraged.

'The trust wouldn't be there.'

'Nor does *that* follow.' He sipped at his sherry, before he continued, 'Charles, you're a very honest man. You don't tell untruths ... even now, you didn't hesitate. You made no denial about having told Richard of our intentions. Not even token denial. Why, therefore, should I disbelieve you when you say you've had second thoughts?'

'David?' I said, doubtfully.

'David need never know about Richard ... indeed, it might be better if he doesn't.'

'Oh!'

'You've changed your mind, that's all.' He smiled. 'A prerogative which is the right of every man ... and part of the—er—mystique of every woman.'

That was Collins. Suave, but not glossy. Superior, but not condescending.

He replaced his glass on the military chest, stood up and said, 'Now ... I'd like your opinion on a new record I've bought. Claudio Abbado and the L.S.O. Prokofiev's ballet music from *Romeo and Juliet.*'

He strolled across the room to his hi-fi, stereo console.

It was some console!

It is deserving of description.

The console itself filled one recess alongside the room's fireplace. It rose from the carpet, to shoulder-height, with neat shelves and alcoves for turntables, cassette and cartridge slots and tape-recording spools. It had everything; from slide-controls to four separate speakers, strategically placed at each corner of the room; from mixers to toggle-switches which, via some electronic magicianship, could record on top of recordings and, if necessary, bring in the V.H.F. radio which was also part of the set-up.

It was (I've already said) Collins's one and only fanaticism ... and who can blame him if he indulged himself.

The equipment did full justice to the recording, and the

recording was good. Of course it was good. Abbado is one of the world's great conductors, and the London Symphony Orchestra is one of the worlds finest assembly of musicians.

But ...

I'd had the argument with Collins before. *Romeo and Juliet* ... probably the most poignant love story ever to leave the mind of a genius. It cried out for music with which to augment its own poetry, and two magnificent composers had ripped their hearts from their breasts and provided that music. Prokofiev and Tchaikovsky.

The world, I think, is divided. The pro-Prokofiev and the pro-Tchaikovsky ... but (except for the musically deaf) there is no anti-Prokofiev and there is no anti-Tchaikovsky. It is a preference—and often no more than a slight preference—every time. Collins (I knew) favoured Prokofiev.

Me?

Let me tell you. Give me that same orchestra—the L.S.O.—and give me Andre Previn wielding the baton, and the Tchaikovsky *Romeo and Juliet* becomes something beyond mere description. It has to be listened to, and to listen to it is to suffer. The love theme ... no artist could ever use colour as Tchaikovsky uses the colours of the various sections of the orchestra. The duel scene, between the fueding Capulets and Montagues ... I swear, Tchaikovsky forces you to see the sparks fly as steel clashes with steel. But the one note—the one bar—of all music is to be found in the Tchaikovsky *Romeo and Juliet*; the saddest, the most heartbroken sound ever to leave an orchestra ... the single, terrible and terrifying chord which denotes the slamming of the vault's door on the two lovers. The final, musical curtain to a love which was always doomed to a pact of suicide.

I am a man who lays no real claim to what are commonly called 'the finer feelings'. In many ways, I am an oaf ... I certainly do not have Henry Collins's capacity for the appreciation of beauty. But that one chord of music moves me. Always! Momentarily, it makes me speechless ... because I am incapable of translating my emotion into words. Momentarily, it brings me close to tears ... *always.*

Which is why I listened to the Prokofiev *Romeo and Juliet,* enjoyed it greatly but, when Collins asked for an opinion, I spoke the truth.

I grinned, wryly, and said, 'Not quite, Henry. Good ... but not quite.'

'Tchaikovsky?' he smiled.

'Still the best. Only fractionally—I'll grant you that ... but still the best.'

'Prokofiev has more majesty ... wouldn't you say?'

'Musically,' I agreed. 'But *Romeo and Juliet* isn't about majesty. Not as I see it. It's about emotion ... and Prokofiev isn't quite emotional enough. Don't get me wrong, Henry. It's great music, and a magnificent recording, but—y'know ... it could, equally well, be incidental music to, say, *King Lear*.'

'Charles,' he chuckled, 'you're a romantic.'

'That'll be the day,' I scoffed.

But, secretly, the remark pleased me, and I took it as a compliment.

'Why?' asked Raff.

I said, 'Eat ... I'll tell you over coffee.'

Raff grunted, and continued to look uncertain.

Raff was suspicious. No—that's the wrong word ... not 'suspicious'. *Unconvinced*. That's better ... he was, as yet, unconvinced. But, given time, and played slowly, it would come. David Raff couldn't mask his thoughts, and his expression showed that he wanted me in, with himself and Collins, but that he hadn't yet fathomed a reason for my change of heart.

That was okay ... I was going to give him a reason. I was going to give them both a reason. A damn good reason which, at the same time, would prove to Gunter that I not only wouldn't double-cross, but that I *couldn't* double-cross.

I'd worked on it, and had come up with a neat trick, but a trick which, to work full-weight, needed telling just once ... twice, and it might have sounded a little threadbare. Which was why (and because Collins hadn't asked) I was keeping the reason under rugs, until after the meal.

We were back at *The Silver Bowl Restaurant*. Same table, same alcove, same waiters ... and I found myself wondering which (or how many) carried the conversation back to Paul Gunter. I even pondered the possibility that the alcove was bugged ... but, on second thoughts, I doubted it.

We'd finished the openers and were half-way through the main dish—Steak Tartare with extras—and I was beginning to have visions of myself as something of a gourmet ... I'd even given the waiter specific, and detailed, instructions concerning the condition in which I liked my steaks.

Ah, well—we can all dream—and it was good food and (anyway) I wasn't paying for it. So why not Walter Mitty things a little?

We talked. We drank good red wine. We chewed our way through the main course, through the sweet and through the cheese and biscuits.

Then, at about nine o'clock (thereabouts) the table was cleared, except for coffee-cups and ash-trays, and we smoked cigars and felt good, and felt warm, and felt companionable ... and (I hoped) felt conspiratorial.

Collins checked that nobody seemed to be listening, then murmured, 'I—er—I think I've come up with something. It may take a few days. Certain details need ...'

'Hold it!' I interrupted, quietly. I glanced at Raff, then said, 'Explanations are called for. David may have lingering doubts.'

'Look—Charlie—if you say ...' began Raff.

'Nevertheless ...' I interrupted. I eased myself forward on the seat, bent my body towards where they sat facing me then, softly, but very deliberately, said, 'Gunter knows.'

'Knows what?' Collins looked puzzled.

'About—y'know ... that somebody's gunning for him. I don't think he knows who. Just—y'know ... *somebody*. And that the "somebody" is a copper. Or, maybe, an ex-copper.'

Raff began, 'How the hell does he ...'

'David,' interposed Collins. He looked at me, and said, 'You're sure of this, Charles?'

'I'm sure.' I nodded. 'He visited me, at the bungalow, this afternoon. Asking questions.'

'The hell he did!' breathed Raff.

Collins said, 'Go on, Charles. We're listening.'

I sent up a quick prayer ... Dear God, let me lie convincingly; let me not falter; keep me close enough to the truth to allow truth to mask that which is not true; guide my tongue—*and let me walk again*.

I kept my voice low and earnest. As sincere, and as ardent, as I knew how.

I said, 'At first—all right ... I thought it was a mad idea. The idea of killing Gunter, and getting away with it. Murder ... and not being caught. I thought it was mad. I said so. All right—I said so ... and, at the time, I thought it *was* mad. Maybe it still is. I dunno. But now, I don't care. It has been done ... undetected murders. They've been committed. Maybe we can do it. Christ Almighty, if *we* can't, nobody can.

'Only—y'know—I didn't think so, at first. Being a copper, I suppose. Knowing what the odds are. What you're up against ... what you're *really* up against. It—er—y'know ... it scared me. It made me think it was impossible. That it couldn't be done. That you were out of your minds. That's why—at first—y'know ... I thought it was a mad idea.'

I paused, and looked at them. I sought expressions of belief, and thought I had found them. I continued, less stumblingly. More sure of myself; more sure of my audience; more certain of success.

I said, 'Gunter came to me, this afternoon. He came to the bungalow. He was waiting, when I arrived home from Susan's place. And he was worried. He tried not to show it—he put on his usual big-shot act—but he was worried. He knows. He's no mug. He knows his skin isn't bullet-proof. He knows he's a damn long way from being immortal, and he knows he *can* be chopped.

'Somebody—I dunno—somehow, he's got wind of things. Not a lot. Nothing specific. No names ... I'm sure of that. But a suspicion that somebody from the force—serving, or ex—has his card marked. It's why he came to my place. To ask, and to proposition me.'

'To proposition you?' said Raff, gently.

'That's why I want in,' I said urgently. 'Two reasons. First—all right, it may sound daft ... but the bastard thought he *could* proposition me. He thinks every man has a price. Every man. Every copper. I find that insulting. Bloody insulting! That an animal like Gunter has me measured as bent. That he thinks I'd take. I find that insulting, David—Henry—I find that bloody offensive, and more than I'm prepared to stand.'

'What was the exact size of the—er—proposition?' drawled Collins.

'Big,' I said.

'Quite. It would be. But, how big?'

I took a deep breath, then said, 'Ten thousand.'

'Christ!' whispered Raff.

Collins said, 'That's a lot of money, Charles.'

'It's a big bribe,' I agreed.

'Why you?' asked Raff.

'He thinks it's cops—or ex-cops,' I explained. 'He thought I might know. Now he thinks I could ask questions ... get to know. He's a worried man,' I added.

'Sure ... but why you?' insisted Raff. 'I mean, why not me? ...'

'After what you threatened to do to his face with broken glass?'

'... Why not Henry? ...'

'The "sea-green incorruptible"?' I said, with a smile.

'... Okay—why not *anybody*? Why, specifically, you?'

Raff. 'The crazy man' according to Paul Gunter. But not so crazy. He was asking the awkward question; the one that had to have a fancy answer tagged to its tail. He wasn't suspicious—don't get me wrong, it wasn't that he disbelieved me—but he was a copper (ex-copper, if you like) and, as a copper, he had to get every tiny strand of a story into a neat and tidy order. And one strand wasn't quite there. That it would come, he didn't doubt ... just that it wasn't yet there. Therefore, he was asking.

'It could be,' proffered Collins, thoughtfully, 'that he saw Charles at the party, the other evening, and noticed that Charles didn't include himself in the—er—incident.'

'It could also be,' I added, 'that when he uses the word "copper"

93

—meaning somebody who's out gunning for him—he means somebody from the city force. His own midden. In which case, he can't be sure who he can trust. With me—I'm ex-county, with a lot of friends in the city ... I'm about as safe as he can get. Maybe his thoughts worked along those lines.'

Raff's eyes narrowed, and he said, 'Us two?'

I looked him a question.

'You've friends in the city force,' said Raff. 'But we're—Henry and myself—we're just about your closest friends. If he's had the tip-off. That *we're* the ones out to even the score ...'

He left the sentence with an open end.

'No-o.' I shook my head, slowly. Thoughtfully. 'We're too close. Surely? He wouldn't take the risk—that I'd pass it on—y'know ... like I am doing, now.'

There was a moment or two of silence.

I was there—I knew it, I didn't have to be told ... I'd sold my two mates the perfect dummy. I only hoped some lunatic in the background was getting it all down, for the edification of Mr Paul Gunter.

I also hoped that, after this evening, I'd be able to learn to live with myself.

Collins sipped his coffee, drew on his cigar, then remarked, 'Ten thousand pounds. That's a lot of money, Charles.'

'One hell of a lot,' I agreed.

'And you weren't even tempted?' His smile spilled over with a mixture of friendly innocence and mild amazement.

'What do you think?' I lied.

'I think,' he said, 'you're to be congratulated. It isn't often a man is given the opportunity to measure friendship in terms of hard cash. Even less often is that friendship not for sale.'

I grunted some sort of reply ... and felt the lowest bastard ever to crawl from the slime under a stone.

Collins said, 'By the way ... what's the second reason?'

'Eh?' I blinked.

'Two reasons for wanting to re-join us,' explained Collins. 'The affront to our friendship ... that's one reason. What's the other?'

I chewed my lower lip for a moment, took a deep breath, then said, 'Because now I think we can get away with it.'

'Really?' Collins showed well-bred interest.

Raff said, 'We always *could* get away with it, Charlie. Henry and I never thought we couldn't.'

'Aye—I know—but ...' I hesitated.

'Go on,' said Collins.

'Look ...' I sought the words; and, this time I really *did* seek the words. 'Let's assume—for the sake of argument—let's assume I take Gunter up, on his offer. Not *actually* take him up, of course ... but kid him along that I've taken him up. I think that would help. Don't you? I think that would make what we all have in mind, not only possible, but safe.'

'I'm sorry ... I don't get it.' Raff's forehead creased as he tried to follow the direction into which I was deliberately pointing his mind.

'Ah, but *I* do.' A slow, knowledgeable smile spread itself across Collins's lips. 'A "third column". That's what you mean ... isn't it Charles?'

I nodded.

'Dicey,' growled Raff. His frown grew deeper, and he added, 'Bloody dicey.'

'Not at all, David.' The enthusiasm grew in Collins's tone. 'What I have in mind. It might take a few days to dovetail all the details. But, if we've a spy in Gunter's camp, we become so much the stronger. Especially if Gunter thinks our spy is *his* spy. Especially if ...' He paused a moment, for thought, then added, 'Ye-es—especially if he knows who we are. I think you should name names, Charles. Tell him who we are—who his executioners are—David and I ... tell him.'

'What the hell!' whispered Raff.

'Why not?' Collins chuckled, quietly. 'It ensures our own safety. Gunter thinks he knows ... therefore he takes precautions. Or, to be precise, what he *thinks* are precautions. He doesn't seek information elsewhere. Why should he? Charles has come up with the perfect answer. More than that—if he plays his cards cleverly enough—Charles might be able to convince Gunter that there's been a change of heart. Then ten thousand pounds *isn't* a bribe to be brushed aside.' Collins looked at me, and said, 'Could you do that, Charles, do you think? Could you make him believe you're now (on the face of things) one of us?'

'I ...' I swallowed, then said, 'I could try. Yes—given luck— I think I could do it.'

'Good.'

Collins didn't rub his hands. The impression was that he was about to do; that, with anybody other than Henry Collins, there would have been a rubbing of hands. That's how delighted he was; how delighted he looked; how delighted he sounded.

Raff was still a dozen lengths behind.

He said, 'Look—I'm damned if I can ...'

'David, let me explain.' Collins used his hands; weaved patterns and counter-patterns in the air with his fingers, while his elbows rested on the table. He drew diagrams; reduced it to single-syllable language, for the benefit of a man whose mind was not given to deviousness. He said, 'First principles. Charles is one of us. Whatever he *pretends* to be—however much he tells Gunter—Charles is, in reality, working for us. Right, now—in order to convince Gunter that, in fact he's working for him— that he's had a change of heart, and is now prepared to accept the bribe—Charles must provide Gunter with information. The better the information, the more Gunter will trust him. The less likely it is that he'll seek either information, or verification of what Charles tells him, from other quarters. Fine ... let Charles tell Gunter that you, and I, are planning his murder. It's true ... therefore it doesn't matter whether, or not, Gunter double-checks. And, after *that* information, Gunter will trust Charles completely.

'Right—so far, so good. Now, let Charles tell Gunter that he's joined us. That, instead of two of us, there are now three of us ... or, at least, that's what you and I think. But let Charles also tell Gunter that this is a ploy. A trick, to ensure that, whatever we plan he'll know about ... and be able to pass on to Gunter. Now, we have him! He thinks he has a spy in our camp whereas, in fact, we have a spy in *his*. We feed him what information we want him to know ... but nothing we *don't* want him to know. We, on the other hand, have complete knowledge of his counter-measures. In the—er—spy trade, this is know as being a double-agent ... that's right, I think, isn't it, Charles?'

'That's what they call 'em,' I said, grimly.

'Subtle,' mused Collins, happily. 'Ve-ery subtle.'

'Bloody dangerous,' growled Raff.

'Oh, I don't think so, David ... not really. And only for a few days. Less than a week, I'd say.' He turned to me, and asked, 'What do you think, Charles?'

'It might work,' I said, gruffly. 'If I can pull the wool over Gunter's eyes ... it might come off.'

Which was how I worked the blinder to end all blinders; by keeping as near to the truth as I dare; by smooth-talking Collins, and allowing Collins to convince David Raff.

By trading upon their absolute faith in me.

Me—Charlie Ripley—double-agent ... who was, in fact a triple agent.

Who was (also in fact) an out-and-out bastard!

-

I remember little about the rest of the evening.

We talked and, gradually, the talk moved away from Paul Gunter and (as I vaguely recall) shunted around books, T.V. programmes and permissiveness in films. The usual subjects. Raff (again, as I vaguely recall) was all for censorship; he wanted some official with the right of veto on all things pornographic; he wanted what he called 'family entertainment'. Collins, on the other hand, argued that censorship—official censorship—was an encroachment upon a man's liberty of choice; that the kinks had as much right to be kinky as the normal people had the right to be normal.

Me? ... I made noises.

The argument was as old as the hills. I could remember when *The Wicked Lady* was a film which sent the Mrs Grundies of the day up the wall ... just because Margaret Lockwood wore a low-cut dress. So Miss Lockwood was (still is) built along the same lines as other women? Big deal! It was a stupid argument then. It still is.

I said so—they both told me that wasn't what they meant ... so I shut up, and let them get on with it.

97

It was raining when the taxi came to collect me. It rained all the way home.

Even the heavens were weeping at this louse who played spitball with his friends.

It was a few minutes after midnight when Gunter phoned. He'd been told. Word-for-word . . . damn near. He knew it all; even that Collins had something in mind.

Gunter sounded pleased with himself. He sounded pleased with me. He sounded as if the whole bloody thing was one huge joke.

He even congratulated me.

I told him to go screw himself, and rang off.

Jesus!

Some men do it for a living. They earn their bread by being scum; by deception and deceit. They can lie—to their friends, and about their friends—and they can still sleep at night.

It can be done.

Like hanging—like throwing the switch of the electric chair—like squeezing the trigger on a firing squad . . . it *can* be done. And, presumably, usage bring some sort of non-feeling. A numbness, maybe. The closing of a metal door. Who knows? . . . maybe even the boredom which normal men occasionally feel about what *they* do for a living.

I wouldn't know.

The only thing I do know is that, not only could I not sleep. I couldn't sit. I couldn't even stand still. Not on that night. I shuffled around the damn bungalow, backwards and forwards—in and out of rooms—like one of those caged big cats you see imprisoned in a crummy zoo. Backwards and forwards—from left to right, then from right to left—shuffling, hobbling, stubbing my shoes against furniture, knocking door jambs with those bloody elbow crutches—like a caged animal . . . but without the beauty of movement nature gives these miserable creatures. I didn't even have that.

In retrospect ...

I'd started by being crippled, physically. Now I was crippled, mentally.

I needed a mental prop; something which would do for my mind what the leg-irons and the elbow crutches did for my body. Something capable of keeping me upright. Some reason, some cause, some banner (however tattered, and however worm-eaten the staff) behind which I could march, and to which I could look, and say, 'This is why! This is my reason and, as far as I'm concerned, a good enough reason.'

I tried Susan.

I told myself. I spoke aloud—talking to myself, almost shouting to myself—and forcing my ears to listen to, and underline, and emphasise arguments which I willed my mind to accept.

I reminded myself that I was a father, and that I had a daughter whom I dearly loved. That (as far as I was concerned, and since her mother's death) she was the most important person on God's earth. That nothing—*nothing!*—was more important than her well-being. That there was no debasement to which I would not commit myself—no humiliation I would not suffer—to ensure her happiness. That, in turn, her happiness depended upon her being whole. That, while she was whole—while she was complete—Chris would love her ... but, if she *wasn't* whole, if she *wasn't* complete? What then?

A wife who couldn't walk? A wife who couldn't stand? A wife dead, from the waist down?

I used Chris as an excuse ... God forgive me, I used a good man as a ready-made excuse for my own weakness!

It worked (more or less) because I willed it to work. I was my own devil's advocate; I told myself (and I forced myself to believe) that no young and healthy man could remain husband, in anything other than name, to dead flesh. And, if the argument was valid (and, at that moment, and as far as I was concerned, it *was* valid) the agony of Susan would be far greater than physical agony. It would be a humiliation and, in time, it would twist and embitter her. Laughter would no longer be part of her make-up.

She would become harsh and angry—with that brand of anger which is an inner thing; which sours and spawns unnecessary and illogical hatreds ... and, in time, she would become the antithesis of her own mother.

For Susan's sake—for Elaine's sake—I forced this crazy pretence upon myself. I made myself believe this stinking untruth—made myself pretend to believe it ... and, by this contemptuous pretence, squeezed some of the self-disgust from my brain.

It was about three o'clock in the small hours when I hit the bottle.

And I hit it hard!

I awoke, flat on my back in the kitchen. I awoke slowly, and with the realisation that I was pinned and, somehow even more helpless than usual. The elbow crutches were beyond reach; in a far corner of the kitchen and with broken crockery and smashed jars surrounding them. I must have hurled them there, in a sudden spasm of drunken disgust ... but, for the life of me, I couldn't remember having done so.

My head hurt, over and above the normal hangover ache. That was there, all right but, in addition, there was a sharp stabbing pain and, when I wriggled my hand to touch the back of my skull, the fingers came away with a slight stain of scarlet. I must have knocked my head when I fell ... but, again, for the life of me, I couldn't remember.

I couldn't remember anything much, beyond the moment when I'd opened the new bottle of *White Horse* ... except (and I remembered this) that I hadn't troubled myself with the unnecessary convention of a glass.

Meanwhile I seemed to be locked, in a horizontal position, on the tiled floor of the kitchen.

I eased myself up on my straightened arms and looked at my legs and feet.

One foot was hooked and caught behind the small-bore copper piping which was part of the central heating system. How it had got there, God only knew—it must have flown and twisted itself, when I'd rid myself of those bloody elbow crutches—but it was there, and it was fast.

It took me twenty minutes to free myself; twenty minutes of cursing, swearing and sweating; twenty minutes of bending forward, twisting and jerking at a useless leg and watching the shoe, inside which was an equally useless foot, stubbornly refuse to be yanked from behind those blasted pipes. Eventually, I lost my temper. I twisted, until I could reach a kitchen stool, gripped the stool by its legs and smashed the apology for a foot loose. I buckled the pipes. I ruined the shoe. For all I knew—for all I felt and for all I cared—I broke every bone in the foot. I felt nothing.

Except, of course, frustration.

I felt *that*! I felt ...

I dunno. How can I tell it? How the hell can I hope to explain to normal, complete men? How can I describe the pointless fury? The helplessness? The sheer, blind rage of those twenty minutes?

All right ... imagine it, if you can.

Then multiply your imagination tenfold.

You are within sight—you are almost within touching distance —of what my feelings were.

I struggled across the kitchen, gathered up my elbow crutches and worked myself into a standing position. I cleaned the kitchen, then moved to the bathroom, shaved and bathed and generally cleaned myself.

Easy—nothing to it ... actions which are certainly not worthy of mention, within a context such as this.

Except, of course, that such actions were not so very simple. They were not so damned 'everyday'. Not with me. They represented almost three hours of hard graft, and a lot of self-disgust.

My foot (when I got around to taking the shoe and sock off) was a little mangled. It was turning pretty colours, and swelling. It wasn't *painful*—it wasn't anything—but it looked messy.

After the bath, I bound it tight in crêpe bandage, used a slipper instead of a shoe and, over the slipper slipped a heavy seaboot stocking ... something I'd last worn when I'd been able to wear waders, stand in a river and fish.

Odd.

Everything I touched seemed to bring back memories. And every memory was a barbed anguish.

I decided to treat myself.

It was Thursday. It was a nice day; one of those sunny, sky-blue days of late spring and early summer. There was a good train service from the nearest station, and Yorkshire were playing at Harrogate. The rain of the night would have made things interesting; with luck, the wicket could have top-dried into a spinner's paradise and, if I got a ripple on, I'd be in time to watch most of the post-lunch play.

Cricket—the most fabulous spectator-sport ever thought up by man ... and, whatever else, I was a 'spectator'.

I decided to stop feeling sorry for myself and, instead, to treat myself.

Let me rapturise a little.

Cricket. Poetry, in sport; the subtleties of chess, played out on a green sward; ballet, with a bat and ball. These (as far as I am concerned) are merely adequate descriptions, not of a sport, but of a near-religion.

I love the game ... probably because I lived through an era of 'the greats'. The pre-war giants. Hedley Verity; the bowler with the perfect length and the immaculate control; the wizard who 'kidded 'em out' by making the impossible look like a doddle. Herbert Sutcliffe; compact and suave, with the collar of his shirt stiffened and standing up at the back of his neck; with his sleeves rolled and folded neatly above the elbows and his pads white enough to dazzle the eyes; an opening batsman whose job it was to break the first attack and who, game after game, did just that and, in doing so, broke the hearts of some of the best fast bowlers in the world. Maurice Leyland; stocky and muscular, and a man who lived for cricket and enjoyed every minute of it; the best middle-order run-getter to stand at a crease; one of the greatest left-handers ever and a man who, whenever he took guard, made the scoreboard tick over like an adding-machine. William 'Big Bill' Bowes; the bespectacled, beanstalk-thin giant who could pluck the middle peg from a batsman's wicket before the be-fuddled batsman had caught sight of the ball in flight; the man who, from the incredible height of his outstretched arm, could deliver a sizzling 'bouncer' or 'yorker' at will; the outfielder who could run, stoop and sling a ball into the waiting gloves of wicket-keeper Wood while the crossing batsmen were yards from their respective creases and already congratulating themselves on a well-placed boundary.

Great men—great Yorkshiremen—and heroes, all. I'd watched them, as a schoolboy and, like every other Yorkshire schoolboy, I'd counted them invincible. And (even taking nostalgia into account) they *were* invincible and, among the many other evils which Hitler was responsible for, the break-up of that superb team is not at the bottom of the list ... not to a Yorkshireman.

I'd watched some of the post-war 'greats'. Truman, Hutton, Wardle and Close. I'd watched, and compared. But none were *quite* as good (not even Truman) and rumours of bickerings in the selection and changing-rooms reached the ears of the followers, and the sourness off the field killed the sparkle on, and the supporters could sense it. For a couple of seasons it was a good side—it could, so easily, have been a *great* side ... but it wasn't.

And now?

We-ell, now it was the Yorkshire County Cricket Club, and a team ... but no-longer *the* team. No-longer the world beaters. No-longer the team the Australians feared even more than they feared the all-England might of a carefully selected test side.

I watched, and saw (or hoped I saw) the germ of a future return to greatness in the play of men, many of whom I was seeing for the first time ... some of whom I'd never heard of. But I watched, and was happy.

*   *   *

I watched, as cricket should be watched; not in the manner of pseudo-connoisseurs who view the game across the open pages of a mental text-book, and with polite applause, but with no deep-rooted pleasure. I watched it from alongside the refreshment tent, with a pint of beer in one hand and a pork pie in the other. I'd dragged one of the chairs into a strategic position, turned it with its back to the field of play, splayed my feet firmly on the uncut grass and rested my backside along the back of the chair. My hands and arms were free; the elbow crutches were leaning against the seat of the chair, behind me.

It was one of those episodes from which future memories are made. The hot sun. The background murmur of voices in the refreshment tent. The green of the outfield, the brown of the wicket and the white figures performing the intricacies of play. The umpire quietly passing another pebble (or, perhaps, a coin) from hand to hand at each delivery. The smell of newly-cut grass. The taste of good beer, mingling with the taste of a pork pie ... a taste which, for reasons I could never fathom, is never *ever* quite the same when the pie is eaten indoors, and from a plate.

Ask me what is heaven and, I will admit, that moments like this must be part of it ... otherwise, for me, it is not heaven.

The man strolled across my line of vision.

He was a middle-aged man, balding and paunchy. He was wearing his shirt loose, outside the waistband of his trousers ... it was a vividly coloured shirt; a kaleidoscopic mixture of reds, whites, yellows and blues. I suppose it was the eye-searing impact of the shirt which first caught my attention.

He was coming from the refreshment tent and, as he passed, I saw the bulging wallet in the back pocket of his trousers, a good half-inch of the wallet was sticking up, beyond the lip of the pocket.

The thought flashed through my mind that this gaudily dressed idiot was one of the 'innocents' of the world; one of the millions of whom every working copper has given up all hope. They are chickens, there to be plucked ... and he was one of them.

I returned my attention to the game in time to see the nearer of the two batsmen drive a badly bowled delivery towards the mid-off boundary. I followed the path of the ball and, again, the fat man wearing the fancy shirt came into my line of vision.

The wallet had gone.

The only man who had passed the fat man—the only person who had been within ten yards of the fat man—was walking towards me. Not hurrying, but walking a damn sight faster than might have appeared at first sight. He was in his late twenties/ early thirties, wearing jeans and a white, open-necked shirt. Long haired and slim ... with slim, sensitive fingers. The fingers of one hand were just leaving the open neck of his shirt.

He was a 'dip'. A pickpocket. A loner. They usually work in groups—two, three and, sometimes, four—one to 'accidentally' bump into the victim while the expert lifts the wallet (or the watch, or whatever happens to be handy), one to take the stolen property from the 'dip' within a sliced second of it leaving its owner's pocket and, sometimes, a fourth man to whom the first 'collector' again passes the property. It gets the loot well clear of the victim before the loss can possibly be noticed and, without the loot, who the hell can prefer charges against either the 'hustler' or the 'dip'?

But, sometimes, the temptation becomes too great. Greed overcomes the natural caution of even the most careful pickpocket ... and this one had the fat man's wallet under his shirt.

I knew it ... damn it, I *knew* it!

I dropped the remains of the pie on to the grass and reached behind me for one of the elbow crutches. As he passed, I bent forward at the waist, and thrust the leg of the crutch between his moving knees.

He went down with a wallop and, as he went down, he snarled, 'What the hell ...'

'The hell,' I said, flatly, 'is that you have another man's wallet under your shirt. The hell also is that this crutch has a steel shaft, and I will have pleasure in parting your hair with it, mate, if I think of you even *trying* to get to your feet.'

In reality, it added up to nothing. A pint-sized crook doing his best to earn a dishonest living; he just happened to have picked the wrong man at the wrong moment ... when a bowler delivered a loose ball, a batsman cracked it towards the mid-off boundary and a man who's spent a lifetime sending tealeaves back to the caddy saw something he'd have been blind to have missed.

It works that way, sometimes.

Sometimes—not often, but sometimes—the cops, too, collect a quota of good luck.

There was a few minutes of lively back-chat. A few naughty words, accompanied by a series of baleful glares. The usual crap ... every copper's heard it, every copper ignores it.

Then a uniformed lad arrived; keen to make an arrest but, at the same time, annoyed that his afternoon's cricket-watching had been interrupted. He took the wallet-collecting comedian in tow, jotted down a few particulars from the dumb bastard who'd had his pocket emptied and made a note of my name and address. Statements were called for and, within the next day or two, one of the local flatfeet would be calling at the bungalow to record my version of what had happened.

Then it was back to cricket.

The fat clown was grateful. He showed his gratitude by buying me another pint, then passed out of my life forever.

It was a nice day—a good game—with a minor incident which lasted a few minutes, and wasn't enough to get excited about.

That's what *I* thought!

'*It's madness ... you realise that?*' said Sullivan, in a harsh voice.

'*Actually, no ... I don't,*' smiled Collins.

'*Crazy,*' insisted Sullivan.

Collins continued to look urbane, and murmured, '*I disagree, Richard. It's neither crazy, nor impossible.*'

'*You're talking about murder, man,*' snarled Sullivan.

'*I'm talking about extermination,*' said Collins, gently. '*I am talking about ridding the world of a man who is mad and, at the same time, powerful. A man who is corrupt, and whose corruption knows no limits. To have rid the world of Hitler, in his youth would, technically, have been "murder". Morally, and on*' the grounds of simple humanity—as we now know—it would have been deserving of the Nobel Peace Prize.'

Sullivan rasped, 'Damn it all, Henry. That's no argument.'

'I find it a very good argument,' countered Collins. 'The canvas is not as large but, in its own way, the one picture is merely a miniature of the other.'

The two men were in the 'Officers' Mess' of the city's Police Headquarters building. The mess was deserted, except for themselves; the grill was across the bar, the glasses had all been collected, washed and stacked after the hour's lunchtime opening.

The bar would open, again, for more social drinking, at six o'clock. Meanwhile, the mess was just about the most private room in the whole complex of this heart of the city's law-enforcement machine.

They sat on hard chairs, opposite each other across a Formica-topped table, and they discussed murder. And one openly admitted that he was going to commit that crime, while the other called him a fool ... but knew that the accusation was untrue.

'I'll stop you,' said Sullivan, grimly.

'You'll try,' agreed Collins. 'I expect you to try ... but you'll fail.'

'All right—let's say I fail ... what about afterwards?'

'Nothing.' Collins shook his head.

'I'll stand you in a dock. I'll send you down for life. I'll not enjoy doing it, but ...'

'Richard.' Collins put patience in his tone. 'You'll need proof. You'll know—you'll know everything ... but you'll still need proof. And that is what you will not have. I'm sorry, Richard, but you won't have proof.'

'Raff ...' began Sullivan.

'David,' interrupted Collins, gently, 'doesn't even know what's going on. If he did—I say this with the greatest of respect—but, if he did, he wouldn't understand. You'd be wasting your time, Richard.'

'Manipulating people,' sneered Sullivan.

'Exterminating Paul Gunter.'

'Manipulating people,' repeated Sullivan, and there was genuine contempt in the words.

'If you like,' sighed Collins. 'Manipulating people ... even you.'

It was a little like returning to the grave; the bungalow was a mausoleum, and I was a zombie, and it was the hour of the cock-crow, and I had been forced to return to the loneliness of my tiny, brick coffin.

For a few hours I'd tasted freedom—albeit shackled freedom ... and a freedom stripped of self-pity. I'd made-believe I was once more a normal creature of the normal world. An ordinary man. A complete man, capable of happiness and capable of content-ment; a man able to laugh and to enthuse—to feel the sun on his skin, and the breeze on his face—to taste good tastes and to enjoy that which other red-blooded men enjoy.

For one moment—one God-given moment!—I'd even become a copper once more ... a copper of a sorts. I'd arrested a villain. A snivelling little two-by-four pickpocket, agreed—a mere tic on the hide of general lawlessness—but, for all that, a hook ... but I'd been able to (and I'd been capable of) arresting him.

And now, back to this.

Back to the leg-irons and the elbow crutches; the makeshift meals and the crumpled discomfort of a rarely-made bed; the solitary misery and the inward turning of bitter thoughts, which always fed on themselves and bloated themselves upon their own bitterness.

Back to this!

Like hell! Like hell (I thought) I will *not* tumble back into the old abyss. I will not allow it to happen; my life may never be eternally bright (but, come to that, whose life ever is?) but it will never again be eternally black. I will fight this thing. I will beat this bloody depression.

Because, you see, I know what my true ailment was ... depression.

Be advised, my friends. Never think you understand; never think you know what true depression is until you, yourself, have suffered it ... because, however good your intentions, and however hard you try, you are *wrong*. You are a million light-years short of what the sufferer can never describe.

I suspect David Raff knows a little of what I mean.

David crawled his way through what polite people call 'a nervous breakdown'. A stupid term—an utterly inadequate term —because what really happens is a mental explosion; a silent bomb-blast under the dome of the skull, which contradicts everything previously accepted as cause and effect and smashes simple logic to hell. There is agony, but no pain. There is a weeping, but no tears. There is a greed for love but, when love is offered, it is turned away. Nobody can help you ... and yet a pea-sized corner of remaining sanity insists that you can never make it alone.

The medics call it Manic Depression. 'Manic' because (as far as they are concerned) it has no known cause; it has no specific start-line; it just *is*, and some people suffer it and some people don't—but the medics are wrong ... because, to the tortured, the moment of snap is as certain and as identifiable as the breaking of an arm (and a damn sight more painful!) but it is such a small thing, and such a stupid thing, that it remains their secret, even under hypnosis. They call it 'Depression' because they can think of no better word. It is as good a word as any, because there is no adequate word. 'Death' might be a better word—or, perhaps, 'Half-Life' ... because self-destruction is never far from the Manic Depressive's thoughts, and to call his sufferings 'Death' would be to invite disaster.

Could be that, as with my own quack, and in the privacy of a consulting room, David Raff's doctor used the term 'Manic Depression' ... using the term as a text-book term, but without even the whisper of a knowledge of what that term really means.

I think David knows.

I knew!

The truth was, it had nothing to do with a smashed spine. It had nothing to do with leg-irons or elbow crutches. It had nothing to do with loneliness or inadequacy. And, strangely enough, it had nothing to do with widowerhood.

These things were *excuses*. They were neat and handy reasons; hooks upon which I could hang the black moods and the savage, all-embracing hatred for the rest of the world. They were 'party-game psychology', if you like ... but they were not the real thing.

None of them was the breaking-point.

Each was a mock-breaking-point, used as a mask for the truth. Because the truth—the *real* breaking-point—was so trivial (so bloody *stupid*!) as to be unbelievable ... but, nevertheless, the truth.

Let me tell you ...

Curtains ... lace curtains

Was there ever such an inadequate reason for insanity?

I was moving into the bungalow. I'd already slept there a couple of nights and, each day Susan (and, when his duties allowed, Chris) came across to lend a hand at the final titivations. Somewhere in the past—weeks before the removal date—we'd discussed the decoration of each room, including the drapes and the chair-covers. We'd decided upon the colour schemes, and we'd chosen the materials.

Susan had suggested lace curtains, and I'd said 'No'. There hadn't been an argument—nothing like that ... just a casual suggestion, and an equally casual veto.

Not that I basically gave a damn. We'd had lace curtains at the windows before, in our lives. On the other hand, we'd *not* had lace curtains. Elaine had decided and, as the spirit had moved her, we had had them, or we had *not* had them. Either way, I'd never given a damn ... nor, come to that, had I given a damn when Susan had made the suggestion. Had she insisted—had she even said, 'Pop, I think you *should* have lace curtains.'—it would have been okay ... lace curtains would have been on the agenda.

That's how unimportant it was.

Then, this day (two days after I'd moved in) she arrived, kissed me 'Hello', took off her coat, unzipped the holdall she'd brought with her and took out lace curtains. All made-up. All ready for fitting. All nice and new.

She held them up for my inspection, and said, 'Well, pop ... what do you think?'

I said, 'I don't want the bloody things,' and I was shocked to find that my voice was tight and hoarse.

She looked perplexed and hurt.

She began, 'They're ...'

'I don't give a damn what they are. I don't give a damn what the *hell* they are!' I exploded. 'They don't belong here. They don't belong in this house. I've already told you. No lace curtains. NO BLOODY LACE CURTAINS.'

I shouted the last words. I screamed them ... and I was scared.

I was scared stupid. I didn't know what the hell was happening to me—why I was doing this—what sort of devil had crawled into me, and was making me act this way. I only knew I couldn't stop myself; that those sodding curtains were, at one and the same time, the least important things in the world, but the most important things of my whole life. I suddenly, and for no logical reason, hated them and wanted to destroy them.

Susan was horrified. Of course she was—who, in her place, wouldn't have been?—she was, without warning, faced with a madman. A maniac whose explosive, maniacal rage had been triggered by such an unimportant thing—by such a trivial thing ... lace curtains.

She gasped, 'Pop ...' then lowered her hands, held the curtains at hip-level and stared at me, slack-mouthed, wide-eyed and terrified.

God alone knows what expression my face carried, at that moment. I sometimes try to think—sometimes try to imagine—but, always, I either can't or daren't. Whatever it was, it frightened my own child; frightened her as I'd never seen her frightened before, or have ever seen her frightened since.

And, understand this—*I wanted to stop* ... but I couldn't!

I stumbled towards her, shouting obscenities at both her and the curtains. When I was within reach, I threw the elbow crutches aside, fell forward, knocked her spinning with my shoulder, grabbed at the curtains and began to rip them into shreds. I sprawled there on the floor, howled insane curses at everything and everybody and tore lace material into tiny pieces until my fingers ached and lost their grip.

I came round ('came round', 'regained my senses', 'brought myself under control' ... use whichever term suits you) an hour, maybe two hours' later. Still sprawled on the carpet. Still clutching shreds of those bloody curtains. And crying.

Sobbing ... and, by that, I mean *really* sobbing. Tears were pouring from my eyes like water from a leaking bucket; the sobs were great hiccups which caught my breath in my throat and almost choked me.

And, again—*I wanted to stop* ... but I couldn't!

It took me another hour to 'cry myself out'. That's the only expression to use—the only expression which fits—'cry myself out'.

Then I hauled myself to my feet, fiddled around trying to pick up the pieces of torn curtain ... and was still doing that when Susan and Chris arrived.

Susan was white-faced, worried stiff and still a little scared. Chris looked grim, puzzled and genuinely concerned.

When they walked timidly into the bungalow, I almost broke down again ... almost.

They were nice people—still are—and they behaved like nice people behave. There was no recriminations. No fault-finding. No criticism. Just an urgent desire to help.

They jollied me into a chair, and forced me to talk. Not to apologise. Not to excuse. Just to talk.

I'll never forget that talk.

'Pop ...' Susan hesitated, then made herself say, 'Pop ... you need to see a doctor.'

'I'm okay,' I mumbled.

'You're *not* okay. Something happened—something terrible ... and you need to see a doctor.'

'Put away?' I asked, in a dull voice.

'Don't be such a bloody fool, Charlie.' Chris stood alongside Susan, and put genuine affection into the remark.

'Why not?' I asked, bitterly. 'I'm obviously mad.'

'Don't be such a bloody fool.'

'You didn't see me.'

'*I* saw you,' said Susan. 'And you're not mad.'

'You can say that? After what I ...'

'After *anything*,' she said, fiercely. 'My father isn't crazy. He's ill—that's all ... he isn't mad.'

'Honey.' I almost strangled on the words. 'I love you—you know that ... I don't have to tell you that. What you've done—what you've both done—and I ...'

'See a doctor, Charlie,' interrupted Chris. 'That's all we want.'

'Why? What the hell can he ...'

'He can help,' insisted Susan. 'We can't—not this time ... we'd like to, but we *can't*.'

'He'll have me certified,' I muttered.

In a very hard, very determined voice, Susan said, 'Over my dead body!'

I looked up at her, and tried to smile my appreciation. Tried to smile the depth of my feelings for her ... and the damn tears almost started, again.

Chris said, 'Charlie, you've had it rough. Bloody rough! You can take so much—only so much ... even you. Then you crack— it boils over ... something like that. It *has* to.'

'You think ...' For the first time I had hope—something which, by stretching the English language to near-breaking-point, you might call hope—and I said, 'You think that's what it was? What it might have been?'

'What else?' asked Chris, sombrely.

Susan said, 'Look—pop—if we don't know what it is, we can't help. It might happen, again. You might—you might—you might ...'

She couldn't say it, so I said it for her.

'Kill somebody?' I said, miserably.

'You might,' she whispered.

'See a doctor, Charlie.' Chris put concerned urgency into the words.

I took a deep breath. They were right—too damn true, they were right—but I was scared. God, was I scared!

Then, in a low voice, I spoke to Susan. I forced her to believe every word ... to understand that I *meant* it. Every word. Every syllable.

I said, 'Don't let them put me away, honey. Whatever it is ... don't let them put me away. Don't let them talk you into it—

please ... whatever they say. Not into a nuthouse. If they say it's needed—if they try to insist—tell me. Just tell me ... that's all. I'll save 'em the expense.'

There was a moment or two of silence. They both knew what I meant, and they both knew I meant it.

Very gently, Chris said, 'We'll tell you, Charlie. You have my word.'

I believed him, and I nodded my thanks.

Susan bent down and kissed me on the cheek.

She said, 'Stop worrying, pop. Stop talking about what isn't going to happen. Just see a doctor ... that's all.'

That's the sort of kid I have. That's the sort of man she married. They don't come bigger ... they don't come finer.

Okay ... I went to a quack.

Okay ... the quack referred me to a skull-shrinker.

The skull-shrinker asked a thousand-and-one stupid bloody question, from whether I still masturbated myself to whether I'd ever peed the bed. Three visits, and I was convinced he was farther round the twist than I'd ever be. He was a poor joke, in bad taste, in a world which, to me had lost all laughter. On the third visit, I told him so ... and told him to keep his questions for fellow-sex-maniacs.

I went back to the quack ... because I'd made a promise to Susan.

The quack consulted notes provided by the skull-shrinker, then went into a long spiel about what happens between the ears. He used the term 'Manic Depression'.

Big deal! I was a Manic Depressive.

He gave me pills—pheno-barbs—and gradually increased the dosage until I was taking two dozen a day. Two dozen! I was walking around like a somnambulist. I didn't know five o'clock from Shrove Tuesday, half the time. I didn't feel low any more ... I didn't feel *anything*.

Then, one day, I muttered, 'Screw this for a life', and slung the pills into the fire.

I had a week of nightmares. A whole week—every night, a personal and private haunting by all the ghouls from hell, all dancing and screaming inside my skull ... then came the daylight.

It was over ... more, or less.

I was normal ... more, or less.

I'd been dragged through Hades by the balls, and I'd survived ... except for a slight case of Manic Depression.

Nothing big, you understand. Just something that started with lace curtains; just something that comes and goes, like the tides; just something I can never rid myself of ... a periodic, gentle, suicidal feeling when everything (even the whites) grey then, for a few hours, become black.

I learned to live with it. I learned to fight it. Sometimes, I even kidded myself I could beat it.

Like that evening ... the evening after the cricket match.

That evening, too, I was going to fight it—lick it, forget it, ignore it, drive it back into its pit ... *anything*!

The usual kidology.

The usual crap.

Gunter arrived at about nine o'clock.

I saw him arrive. I was on the window-seat of the bungalow's living-room bay, watching the deepening colours of a smoked-salmon sky to the west, puffing gently on a perfectly-packed pipe and listening to a cassette of Mozart's Fortieth—the real thing ... not the popped-up version. The eyes, the ears, the mouth; each adding its own special ingredient to a sweet mix of contentment ... then the Peugeot drew up at the gate.

Gunter was being chauffeured; the goon behind the wheel was just that ... a goon. Thick-limbed. Short-crop-haired. Heavy-browed. You meet them; in the force you meet them all the time. There is a factory, somewhere, where they stamp them out, like so many plastic mugs; each identical; each overloaded with beef; each short on brain-mechanism; each cheap and nasty; each destined to be a 'soldier' in the army of some 'Mr Big'.

One of Gunter's could drive a car.

The goon stayed in the driving seat. Gunter walked up the path, came into the bungalow and, a couple of seconds later, was in the room with me.

I'd turned my head to watch him enter the living-room.

'They've been invented some time,' I growled.

'Eh?'

'Doors,' I explained.

'What about doors?'

'You are,' I explained, 'expected to knock on them. Force yourself ... it comes easier with practice.'

'Don't make cheap cracks,' he sneered. 'I have to see you.'

I said, 'No crack is cheap ... not when you need an expensive motor car to get within listening distance.'

He glanced around the room, and said, 'Where d'you switch this damn thing off?'

'Leave it.'

'I want to talk to you, Ripley.'

'It isn't important,' I said.

'How the hell ...'

'Mozart wrote this thing,' I said harshly. 'Mozart was not a bastard—you *are* ... therefore, whatever you have to say is of secondary importance to this music.'

'Up you, Ripley.' He spotted the radio/cassette-player, strode across the room, pressed the 'Off' switch, and said, 'Up Mozart.'

The silence was much louder than the music had been. Out to the west a cloud—a long, thin, purple-black scarfe—drifted across the salmon sky.

Gunter walked towards the bay. There was an armchair, positioned at an angle, with its back towards the window-seat. Gunter used it. He relaxed; not watching me, but knowing that I could see his face from a back-and-to-one-side view.

He said, 'You played hero today, Ripley.'

He'd killed the music, so I let him do the talking.

'At Harrogate.'

'I was at Harrogate, today,' I admitted.

'You played hero,' he grunted.

116

'I watched a cricket match ... that was the only important thing I did at Harrogate.'

'That wallet,' he said, softly.

'A man had his pocket picked,' I conceded. 'There was a wallet in his pocket.'

'The fatso.' He tilted his head slightly, looked at a corner of the ceiling, and spoke in a gentle, sing-song tone. He said, 'The fatso was careless. His wallet fell out of his pocket. A man saw it —picked it up—was on his way to take it to the cops, when you played hero ... there was a misunderstanding.'

'You want to know the "misunderstanding", Gunter?' I said. 'Your pal made it. He picked the wallet up, before it fell ... right?'

'Not *my* friend,' explained Gunter, smoothly.

'Of a kind,' I growled.

'The friend of a man I owe a favour to.'

'That's your worry ... you still owe it.'

Gunter smiled at the cornice. A confident smile; an assured smile; a slow smile which brimmed over with absolute certainty.

He said, 'He'll be up, tomorrow ... before the beak. A remand. He'll ask for bail ... he'll get it. A fortnight—three weeks—he'll be tried ... you'll give evidence, Ripley. You're the star witness. The only *real* witness. You saw him stoop ... on second thoughts, you saw him bend down and pick something up. It might have been the wallet. You're not sure ... but it *might* have been the wallet. That's all you have to say.'

My lip curled, and I sneered, 'Is that all?'

'Not much. A little doubt.' He turned his head, and looked at me, then said, 'The legal terminology is "reasonable doubt" ... that's all.'

'Go screw yourself, Gunter,' I snarled.

'You will.' He chuckled, then added, 'And the other thing ...'

'What "other thing"?'

'Come on, Ripley ... come *on*.'

I choked on my own helplessness, then muttered, 'All right. What about the "other thing"?'

'The room's already booked.' He pushed himself from the chair as he spoke.

'What room?'

'At the Swiss clinic.'

'Oh!'

'All you have to do is earn it ... eh?'

I nodded. Once. I couldn't trust myself to speak.

He reached the door, turned, then said, 'And the "reasonable doubt" thing. Let's call it a bonus ... it'll buy you a pair of shoes.'

He left. I watched him walk down the path; watched him climb into the rear of the Peugeot; watched the goon work the ignition and turn the steering-wheel; watched the car drive down the road, and out of sight.

The purple-black cloud had thickened to fill almost half the sky. Most of the salmon tints had been replaced by blood-scarlets striated with pus-yellows and putrescent-greens. It was beautiful ... but evil-looking. Magnificent in its perfect reflection of corruption.

It was dusk ... and almost dark.

So, why not?

For Christ's sake, *why* not?

I'd drawn the curtains and switched on the lights. I'd started the cassette, but Gunter had pressed the 'Off' switch only a few bars from the end of the first movement, and the second movement was no companion to my present mood, therefore I'd changed cassettes—to the favourite—to the one that always helped —to the Tchaikovsky *Romeo and Juliet* ... turned low, and to be mere incidental and background music to my thoughts.

Some thoughts!

But realistic—that's what I told myself ... *realistic*.

I'd done a first-class stripping job. I'd stripped myself mother-naked—not of clothes, but of pre-packed opinions and ready-wrapped beliefs—and now I was having a damn good look at myself. I was shoving a spy-glass into every aperture and prodding every wart. I wanted to see. I wanted to be sure. I wanted the truth ... whether it was rose-scented or whether it stank like a bad fart.

Just the truth ... that's all.

And the truth was, that I was going to do it. So who the hell was I kidding? And the truth was that corruption was corruption, and that corruption was not for sale at various prices or in various sizes. You took the world, or you had nothing. There was no 'sample packs'.

Okay—start with that proposition, and everybody is corrupt ... everybody! Everybody is a Judas; everybody is on the take; everybody is busy running his (or her) own private little 'Watergate'.

It is happening. Take Collins. Take Raff. Take Sullivan. Three very nice blokes. Honest. Straight. They do not come any cleaner and, if *they* are on the take, everybody is on the take. They are on the take ... believe me.

Collins has a hi-fi, stereo set-up. The best. He loves his music, and he pampers himself by making damn sure that the music he loves is delivered via as near to perfect reproduction as electronic magic will allow. The set-up is the best—which means it is expensive ... but five-per-cent less expensive than it would be to some man not wearing police uniform. I know this ... I know it, because I, too, have used the same store, and there is a standing arrangement. Five-per-cent discount for all cops.

Raff uses the store.

Sullivan uses the store.

Nor is it the only store ... not by a few dozen!

There are cafes, where the first copper has to pay for a cup of tea, or a sandwich. There are cinemas where, to coppers and their wives, the best seats are on the house. There are boozers, where coppers sit in The Lounge, but pay Tap Room prices. At every Police Dance, there are prizes—spot-prizes, raffle-ticket prizes, beat-the-band prizes—more prizes than *that* ... all donated by 'grateful' shopkeepers and tradesmen.

The list goes on, and it is a long list. Nothing huge. Everything small. But a lot of littles make a big ... and corruption only comes in one size.

So, who the hell *isn't* corrupt?

Or are you, maybe, saying that the five-per-cent off—the free cups of tea—the free cinema seats—the cheap booze—the umpteen prizes are all there because *everybody*—everybody—loves a copper? That our policemen really *are* 'wonderful'?

And, if you say 'Yes', who the hell is kidding who?

So-o ...

All Gunter is is open. He is honest ... honest about his own graft. Which at least makes a pleasant change.

Gunter's graft is a means to an end. It is there for a purpose, and a very specific purpose and, without that purpose, it would not be there. Gunter wouldn't waste either time or money corrupting somebody he hadn't already lined up for some use.

Which makes him better—bigger—than all the small-time grafters.

The ones I'm talking about.

Their graft is the 'just-in-case' graft. Just in case this particular copper sees my car parked on a double-yellow line. Just in case I forget to sign my driving licence—forget to buy my dog licence —forget to check the clock, before I pull the last pints—wash my car when there is a water-shortage—nudge my way past the speed limit—sell cigarettes to some kid whose age I have not checked ... just in case.

I have news for these small-time berks. Screw the cops—pay the fine ... in the long run, it's a damn sight cheaper.

And, whatever Gunter is, he is not two-bit. He is big. He is a bastard ... but he is a *big* bastard!

The truth—that night—when I stripped away layers of pretence, like stripping away the layers of an onion and, at last, reached the tiny green heart. The bitter centre. The part that tasted sour, but the part all the other parts masked.

That (damn him to hell!) I hated Gunter—I loathed and detested every drop of blood in his veins, and every fibre of flesh on his body ... but (damn him to hell!) I also *admired* him.

He was an animal, but he was a *complete* animal.

He was honest—more honest than lesser men would dare to be —more honest than any other man I'd ever known. His corruption was on such a grand scale that it became magnificent—monu-

mental—and, by its very size, almost ceased to be corruption ...
became, instead, near-diplomacy.

That was a truth I touched, that night.

That, let the villainy be great enough, and the villain can
rightly claim heroic stature.

Susan phoned, as usual, at just before eleven. It was a very oddball
conversation. From her end, it must have sounded particularly
screwy—full of senseless innuendoes, and remarks without meaning
... but they *had* meaning, and I wish she could know what I was
trying to say. I think she might understand.

The conversation went like this ...

'Hello, pop. How's things?'

'Fine. Fine.'

'Nice weather. What's it been like over there?'

'Nice. I—er—I treated myself to a day out.'

'Really?'

'Harrogate.'

'Harrogate?'

'Uhu. Yorkshire were playing. I—y'know—suddenly got the
urge to watch some decent cricket.'

'Good ... I approve.'

'Tell Chris. With luck, we should have a good team. Within
the next few seasons.'

'I'll tell him. He'll be pleased. Y'know, pop—you should do
things like that more often.'

'Uhu. Maybe.'

'You *should*.'

'I'll think about it.'

'Pop ... is there anything wrong?'

'No. Why should there be?'

'Your voice ... that's all.'

'What's wrong with my voice?'

'Nothing—not really, I suppose—just that ... Anyway, you
enjoyed the cricket.'

'And arrested a pickpocket.'

'So you'll ... You did *what*?'

'Arrested a pickpocket.'

'Honest?'

'Cross my heart.'

'How did *that* happen?'

'I was there—by the refreshment tent—and this man passed, with a wallet in his hip pocket. Then this other bloke—typical tea-leaf—lifted it. I saw it happen.'

'And you *arrested* him?'

'Uhu. I tripped him up, and threatened to brain him with one of my crutches.'

'Good for you, pop. Good for you!'

'Honey ...'

'Yes?'

'He—er—he *did* steal that wallet.'

'Of course he did. If you saw it ...'

'I mean—y'know ...'

'What?'

'He *did*.'

'Look—I don't know what you're getting at. Of course ...'

'I mean—if he's acquitted.'

'Is it likely?'

'I dunno. Maybe.'

'You mean there's some doubt?'

'No. No doubt.'

'All right. What's worrying you?'

'Just that, if he is acquitted. You'll know. I wasn't mistaken. He *did* steal that wallet.'

'Okay. So, why *should* he be acquitted?'

'They—the courts—they don't always ... y'know. Sometimes, they see a doubt. One that isn't there. Sometimes.'

'From what you say, there *isn't* any doubt ... is there?'

'No. No doubt.'

'Well, then. Pop, I'm proud of you. Honestly—to do a thing like that ... I'm proud of you.'

'Don't ...'

'What's that?'

'Don't ... Y'know—don't ever *not* be, honey.'

'What?'

'I couldn't stand that.'

'Pop ... are you okay?'

'Uhu. I'm—y'know ... I'm okay.'

'You sound as if ...'

'What's that?'

'You're not *crying*, are you?'

'C-crying?'

'You sound as if ...'

'Don't be stupid, honey. I don't cry. I'm not ...'

'You sure?'

'Look—why the hell should I ...'

'Are you all right, pop? Are you feeling all right?'

'Certainly ... certainly I'm feeling all right.'

'Sure?'

'Sure.'

'Look—don't be a bloody martyr, pop. If you're feeling rough ...'

'I'm *not* feeling rough.'

'All right. Only ...'

'Be told.'

'All right. All right. Only ...'

'Honey, you're as bad as your mother.'

'What?'

'Your mother. She was always worrying herself. You're as bad as *she* was.'

'Because we both think you're pretty important. She did. I still do.'

'For God's sake, honey!'

'Is that a crime?'

'No ... no, it's not a crime. But ...'

'Be grateful, pop. Don't knock it. A lot of people ...'

'I know. I know!'

'So, be grateful.'

'I'm—I'm grateful. God knows, I'm grateful.'

'Pop! I'm only kidding. I—I didn't mean you to ...'

'*I'm* not kidding, honey.'

'Please, pop! There's something wrong, isn't there?'

'Nothing.'

'Pop, you're lying.'

'I've—I've been out all day. Watching cricket—arresting thieves ... I'm a bit pooped. That's all.'

'I wish I could believe you.'

'That's all.'

'I—I wish I could be sure.'

'That's all ... I'm tired.'

'D'you—d'you want me to come over?'

'Why the hell should you ...'

'Chris'll run me over. It won't take more than ...'

'No!'

'Pop, there's something the ...'

'Honey, I'm tired. That's all. I've had a big day, and I'm tired. I'm going to have a bath, brew some hot tea, have a bit of a read —maybe listen to some music for a while ... then I'm going to bed. Now, that's all ... believe me. Don't be like a mother hen.'

'You're sure?'

'I'm sure.'

'Because ...'

'I'm *sure*.'

'Okay ... if you say so.'

'Goodnight, honey. Thanks for ringing.'

'Goodnight, pop. God bless.'

'God bless, honey.'

That damn telephone conversation. The number of times a bloody phone breaks down; you can't say something important— something you want to say ... something that needs saying. But, when you're there, saying things you shouldn't be saying. When you're making stupid noises you shouldn't be making. Bet your shirt on it ... that's when the bloody phone works perfectly!

That damn telephone conversation.

She didn't understand it. I didn't understand it too well, myself. All it did was make the poor kid worry.

And all *that* did was make two of us.

1 did what I said I was going to do. Not because I'd planned it. Not because of anything—other than that that's what I'd told Susan I was *going* to do ... and, insignificant though it was, I wanted to keep faith with her in *something*.

A stupid reason?

Maybe. In that case, I had a bath (because I was stupid), then I brewed hot, sweet tea (for a reason other than being stupid), and I hauled myself to an armchair—the armchair Gunter had used —and opened a book (again, for a reason other than being stupid).

To have a bath, I'd had to get undressed. I'd taken off the seaboot stocking, then the slipper, then the sock, then the crêpe bandage ... and then I'd seen the foot.

Judas Christ!

It scared me, more than a little.

It didn't look like a foot any more. It was twisted and broken, and there was the jagged end of smashed bone sticking out of one side. It was seeping blood—the crêpe bandage and the sock were both sticky with the stuff—and the colours matched the colours of that sunset I'd watched after Gunter had left.

I washed it, in the bath, and the sponge snagged against the end of the bone, and I wanted to puke. Not from pain, but because ...

Hell. Use your imagination!

Let me tell you a little thing about being dead from the hips down. Something a lot of people forget. Something even *I'd* forgotten.

That you can die down there—and I mean really die—and not know it. There is no pain ... there is no *anything*! Your leg could be sliced off, at the knee, and you would know nothing, until you fell sideways.

No pain—no feeling ... therefore, you are out of touch.

Think about it. I am not asking for sympathy, but just think about it. Pain. It hurts, but it hurts for a reason. To draw attention to itself; to let you know that something is on the tilt. You cut yourself; the pain lets you know, and warns you not to use that part until the flesh has healed. You break a bone; the pain sends signals, and makes damn sure you keep pressure away from the fracture until the bone has knitted. You pull a muscle, you twist a joint, you bruise yourself ... pain lets you know, and pain warns you off.

Take away the pain and you are in *real* trouble.

You keep using a part that is already smashed. Like at a cricket match. Like when you arrest a pickpocket.

Judas Christ!

I'd been warned. Everybody who ends up without feeling in the southern hemisphere gets the same, stern warning. Anything can happen—gangrene can take over—and the mortician is screwing down the coffin lid, before you get the message. It has happened ... and not a few times.

And by the look of my foot, it was going to happen again!

I brewed hot, sweet tea, laced it with brandy and felt the lip of the mug rattle gently against my teeth as a quick burst of shakes took over. That's how scared I was; that damn foot might have to come off ... maybe the whole leg. Then 'Goodbye, Swiss clinic.'—even 'Goodbye leg-irons and elbow crutches' ... and 'Hello, wheelchair.'

I drank the tea, while I talked myself out of picking up the telephone and yelling for an ambulance to come and take me to the nearest hospital.

I didn't want a hospital. I was horse-trading for *more* freedom, not less. Those damn medics—those damn surgeons—they were too eager to do a butchering job ... they were too damn eager with a knife. I wanted all of it there—both legs, both feet—so that, when the Swiss whiz-kid worked magic on my spine, it would mean something.

I even did something I hadn't done for a long, long time ... I prayed. And, what is more, I meant it.

I worked hard to screw certain beliefs into myself. That, as a layman, I didn't know what the hell I was talking about (which was true enough) and that, to a layman, an injury always looks worse than it is. That the human body can take some stick and, with nothing more involved than rest, can mend itself.

I didn't need a doctor ... that's what I told myself.

I could heal my own body ... that's how crazily I argued.

That I eventually believed myself is, I suppose, a measure of my desperation. A measure, if you like, of my yearning for those few remaining years of 'completeness' and a fear that my own momentary lack of self-control had robbed me of those years.

I did something of which, in my own pig-headed way, I was proud ... of which (and for the same reason) I am still proud.

I hauled myself to the clothes-closet and took the wheelchair from its hiding place. I sat in it and, by bending and wriggling, positioned a cushion on the foot-platform and rested my mangled foot on the cushion. Then I wheeled myself around the bungalow, collecting the items I would need. Antiseptic. Cotton-wool padding. Bandages. Surgical tape An old slipper, which I slit down one side. The twin to the seaboot stocking I'd taken off.

And the brandy bottle. I had a feeling I might need the brandy bottle, before I was through.

I didn't—not until I'd finished ... and, of this, too, I was stupidly proud.

The bad moment was when I had to force the protruding bone back into position; back beyond the ripped skin and torn flesh, and to where I thought it should be. There was no pain, but my imagination provided a silent echo of the torture which was missing and, with my trembling fingers, I felt rather than heard the broken ends of the bone touch and jag against each other. Then I kneaded the foot into what I thought a foot should look like, doused the result in antiseptic, padded it with cotton-wool, bandaged it, then strapped it, tight, from ankle to toes, with surgical tape.

It was messy; the damn thing started bleeding badly as I manoeuvred the bone into position and, before the cotton-wool padding was in place, the cushion was soaked. Nor did I know too much about antiseptics; I had a vague fear that too little would

127

be insufficient to kill the germs, but that too much might burn, and do harm to, the healthy flesh. The constriction of the sugical tape was something else I had to consider; tight enough to hold it immobile, but not so tight as to prevent the circulation of healing blood.

It was one hell of a situation. 'Touching toes', the hard way. And, before the surgical tape was in place, the sweat was dripping from my chin and from the end of my nose.

I gave myself a few minutes breather, then eased the slit slipper into position. Taped it in place with more surgical tape, replaced the ruined cushion and finally pulled on the seaboot stocking.

At least it *looked* okay—more, or less—and, as far as I was concerned, it was going to stay like that for a week. Maybe a fortnight. That was another thing I wasn't too sure about. The time it took for bone ends to fuse together ... what was too little, and what was too much.

It was all hit and miss, and without even the guidance of an increase, or a decrease, in pain.

Then I cleaned up the mess, wheeled myself to the bathroom, washed my hands and (only then) took a long, hard swig from the brandy bottle.

Then, back into the living room and a hauling job to get myself from the wheelchair and into the comfort of the armchair. A cushion under the injured foot, a book ... and (as I saw things) patience and crossed fingers.

The book—a paperback edition of 'Hemingway By-Line'—was an unconscious, but very appropriate choice.

Great writing—great reporting—hiding behind a mask of easy-reading. The one-and-only Ernest Hemingway; a man who could say things other men felt, but could never put into words; a man who could, so easily and so much better, have told this thing as it happened ... so much better, and so much simpler.

And, again ... Collins.

Henry had introduced me to books. Real books. Good books. As a kid—as a teenager—I'd ploughed my way through 'required reading'. Dickens, the Brontë sisters, Mark Twain, Conan Doyle —a dozen, or so, other distinguished authors ... some of which I'd enjoyed, but some of which I'd counted as heavy going, and so much wasted time. Then, when I'd joined the force, I hadn't had too much time for books. Westerns, Second World War yarns, biographies and autobiographies—usually (as I now realise) ghosted and guyed up to make a dull life sound interesting ... that had been my steady literary diet for almost a quarter of a century.

Then the bullet had chipped my spine.

I'd tired of radio, and I'd tired of television, and (at the time) I was on my back, with the expert's promise that 'perpendicular' was a position I might dream about, but could never achieve.

And, gradually, Henry had weaned me away from the ocean of self-pity, via (among other things) books. He'd chosen them for me. Shaw ... not the plays, but the *Prefaces*. Priestley—again, not the plays, or the novels, or the massive non-fiction works, but the small pieces ... the essays and the articles. Chandler—odd, I'd heard of Chandler, but never read him ... which was fine, because I was suddenly made aware of what could be done by fusing fine words with a comparatively simple cops-and-robbers yarn.

And Hemingway ... Henry Collins had introduced me to Ernest Hemingway.

The man who was *all* man, but also an artist. The man who wrote *for* men, but without a put-on 'masculinity'; who'd experienced everything—war, bull-fighting, big-game hunting, the lot—and who was capable of translating his experiences into words ... of taking the reader into battle, and into the bull ring, and into the jungle as truly, and as completely, as if the reader really *was* there.

But with compassion and with poignancy. And, sometimes, with bitterness ... a bitterness which (in those days) I understood.

It is possible (it is more than possible, knowing Collins) that Henry was well aware of the eagerness with which I might grasp Hemingway's philosophy; that this author, of all authors, might pass some of his own rugged strength—some of his own mountain-sized determination—onto me, via the magic of his prose.

It worked.

Other authors I enjoy, but Hemingway I love. Especially the articles—the by-lines—which are a distillation of high moments in the life of a man who was also an artist ... but, above all else, a *man*.

I awoke. Still in the armchair, still in pyjamas and dressing-gown, and still with Hemingway open, on my lap.

I glanced down at my foot.

Maybe the lower part of the leg, just above where the tape ended, wasn't quite as swollen as it had been the night before. Maybe it wasn't—maybe it was ... I couldn't decide.

I trundled into the bathroom. Washed and shaved (in a sitting position) then rolled the wheelchair into the kitchen and fixed myself some scrambled eggs, toast, marmalade and strong coffee.

I returned to the living room. Climbed back into the armchair, folded the wheelchair and (by contorting myself backwards and sideways) secreted the damn thing behind the drawn-back, floor-length curtains of the window.

I had my pipe and tobacco. The telephone was within reach. I could, by twisting my head, see anybody walking up the path and to the door. I had books.

I was going to sit this damn thing out.

I was going to give that bloody foot time—a week, a fortnight, if necessary—to make some sense of itself.

Dick Sullivan arrived, mid-morning.

I'd heard the gate, turned in the armchair, spotted the parked Rover and seen Sullivan walking up the path. When the bell buzzed, I'd yelled, 'Come in', and he'd come in ... now, he entered the living room.

He stopped, just inside the door, and said, 'What the hell?'

'Nothing.' I shrugged. 'I ricked my ankle a little, that's all.'

'Badly?' He sounded worried.

'No-o,' I lied. 'Just a twist. A couple of days, and it should be okay.'

As he closed the door, he said, 'What does the doctor say?'

'Nothing ... he doesn't know.'

'That's a bit stupid, isn't it?'

'Rest. That's all it needs. That's what it's getting.'

'How does Susan feel about it?' He crossed the room, stood in front of me, and stared down at the foot resting on the cushion. 'She'll be worried.'

'If she knew, she might worry,' I admitted. 'She doesn't know ... and I don't *want* her to know.'

'Charlie, you really ought to ...'

'Forget it,' I cut in irritably. Then I grinned and, in a more reasonable voice, said, 'Forget it, Dick. It's nothing. Just a sprain ... that's all. A couple of days, and it'll be as good as new.'

He sighed, heavily, and nodded. He wasn't too happy, but he wasn't going to argue.

I said, 'Take a seat. There's some beer in the fridge.'

'No beer.' He bent himself onto a chair alongside the fireplace. He said, 'I'm here on business.'

'Gunter?' I asked.

'That, too,' he agreed.

'Something else?'

'We'll come to it, later.' He felt in his pockets for pipe and tobacco. 'Meanwhile ... what about the daft idea Collins and Raff are cooking up?'

'Nothing new,' I lied.

'No?' He was using flake tobacco and he folded a flake, placed it in the palm of his left hand and, with a steady, rolling movement of his right thumb, teased it into shreds. It was a perfect mortar-and-pestle movement. He murmured, 'I thought you'd have been back in there, Charlie ... like I asked.'

'After you'd warned Collins?' I countered quizzically.

'You didn't even try?'

'Oh, yes ... I tried.'

'And?'

I said, 'If I tell 'em the time of day, they'll check their watches.

That's how much they trust me.'

'As bad as that?'

'What d'you think?'

'I think,' he said, slowly, 'that Henry Collins is a very cunning old fox. I think he may be doing something you don't know about.'

'Or nothing,' I ventured. 'After you've given him the "Keep Off" routine.'

'Something you don't know about, Charlie,' he repeated, gently. He looked up from the tobacco, and said, 'You'd tell me? If you knew anything, you'd tell me?'

I nodded.

He said, 'For everybody's sake.'

'For everybody's sake,' I agreed.

He nodded, as if satisfied, returned his attention to the tobacco, packed and lighted his pipe, then said, 'The dip.'

'Oh! The—er—dip.'

'It's why I'm here ... officially.' He grinned. 'It's an excuse. To ask about the other thing.'

'Assistant Chief Constable (Crime).' I returned the grin. 'On enquiries about pickpockets. Things are looking up.'

'It's an excuse.' His grin widened. 'It gets me out of that damned office ... and, with my rank, who argues?'

'Who argues?' I agreed.

'What happened?' he asked.

I told him. Exactly what had happened; chronologically, and without frills. I told him *exactly* what had happened.

He listened, smoking his pipe and grunting his approval at all the appropriate spots.

I finished the telling, and he said, 'Good. I've got the details. I'll have a statement typed out, and get somebody to call and ask you to sign it.'

'There's—er—one thing,' I said, hesitantly.

'What's that?'

'He could have picked it up.' I forced myself to say it and, having said it, knew that it was stick-or-bust from now on.

'Picked what up?' he asked, with a frown.

'The wallet?'

132

'Picked it up?'

'From the grass. From the ground.'

'Sorry ... I don't follow.' The frown narrowed his eyes and creased his forehead.

'There was a moment, when I wasn't watching. Y'know ... I was watching the game. The wallet could have slipped out of the fat man's pocket.'

'Did it?'

'I don't know ... but it *could* have done.'

'And?'

'Well—y'know ... he could have picked it up.'

'The tea-leaf who nicked it?'

'Aye. *If* he nicked it.'

'He nicked it,' said Sullivan, in a flat voice.

'We can't be sure. We can't ... '

'*I'm* sure.'

'Oh!'

'With *his* previous convictions. As long as your arm. Don't worry, Charlie, he nicked it.'

'I'm not worrying. It's just that ...' I stopped. I might have waved my arms. I didn't; I forced myself not to.

'Just *what*?' he asked, softly.

I said, 'The magistrates won't know.'

'What won't they know?'

'That he has form. That he's a villain.'

'They'll be told.'

'Aye ... but after he's been convicted.'

'Meaning?'

'*If* he's convicted.'

He took his pipe from his mouth. Slowly. He watched my face. He said, 'Just what are you getting at, Charlie? That he *won't* be convicted?'

'He—er ...' I couldn't look at his—not directly into his eyes—when I said, 'There's an element of doubt. He's entitled to it.'

'Bullshit,' he said, gently.

'Dick, he could have picked that wallet up. From the ground. He *could*.'

'True. I could set fire to this bloody bungalow. I could light

133

my pipe. Drop the match onto the carpet. Set fire to the bungalow. I *could* ... but it's a million-to-one I won't.'

'You don't believe me,' I said, tightly.

'I believe you,' he growled. 'If you weave this sort of crap in the witness box, the magistrates'll believe you. He'll get away with it. But there has to be a reason.'

'For him getting away with it?'

'For you changing your story, Charlie. For you arresting a man—being so damn sure, at the time—arresting him, then telling an unvarnished yarn to the copper, when it happened ... and now this.'

'I'm telling the truth,' I snapped.

'You're twisting the truth.'

'Like hell. I'm ...'

'You are giving a thief a loophole,' he said, deliberately. 'You— an ex-copper—an ex-chief superintendent—you're giving an habitual villain a way out. You know it ... you know bloody well. Get up in a witness box. Tell 'em you've had—what is it, "second thoughts"?—and we've all been wasting our time. It's what makes crime pay. God damn it, Charlie, I don't have to tell you. I don't have to tell *you*.'

'A tin-pot little dip,' I said, bitterly.

'So, why change your mind?'

'And it needs an Assistant Chief Constable (Crime).'

'I've already told you why.'

'And bent evidence.'

'Nobody's asking you to tell ...'

'Just a little bent. Just a *leetle* bit.'

'Don't accuse me of that,' he snarled. 'Not you ... *you* of all people.'

'And what the bloody hell is *that* supposed to mean?'

At that moment, we hated each other. Dick Sullivan and Charlie Ripley; cops who had worked together—who had waged war against the crooks, side by side—men much alike in their ways and in their manner of thought ... even in their manner of speech. And, at that moment, we loathed each other.

He knew—damn right he knew ... something! He didn't know what. He didn't know why. Or who. But he knew *something* had happened. A man with a quarter of a century of practical coppering behind him—a man who knows the law, and the weaknesses of the law—a man who's despised (and still despises) every bent bastard walking the face of the earth ... that sort of a man doesn't deliberately open a door and allow an insignificant germ of a pickpocket to run free. Not unless there's *something*.

Dick Sullivan knew ... he just didn't know what.

I knew.

I knew a fine (maybe three months, inside) wasn't going to stand between what I was and what I might become. If a pint-sized thief had to run loose in order that I might walk again, that was okay by me. There was no decision—no question ... not the ghost of a prayer!

But Sullivan didn't know that—he didn't know the stakes—therefore at that moment, he hated me.

And I hated him back, because he thought so little of me; he thought—he *must* have thought—that my price was contempt-uously cut-rate ... he didn't even know me better than *that*!

He stood up from the chair and, in a flat, unemotional voice, said, 'I'll get the statement typed out.'

'Aye.'

'Including the—er—"freedom clause".'

'As it happened,' I growled. 'Everything.'

'I'll send it out. You can sign it.'

'After I've read it.'

'After you've read it,' he echoed, grimly.

'I'll sign it ... if I agree with it.'

'Aye.' He walked across the room, glanced at my foot, then said, 'Take care of that ankle.'

'It'll be right.'

As he opened the door, he said, 'Just don't be bloody stupid in *all* things, Charlie ... that's all.'

He left, and I twisted my head to watch him walk down the path. I watched him climb into the car, and watched the car drive away.

And I suddenly felt lonely ... bloody lonely.

I was on my backside, in an armchair. Pinned, and helpless. More helpless that I'd even been with the leg-irons and elbow crutches. More helpless, even, than the wheelchair made me. I was part *of* the chair. I was the most crippled bastard on God's earth. Physically crippled, and mentally crippled. Mentally crippled, because I had worries I couldn't share, and secrets I couldn't tell. Nasty secrets ... and worries which were driving me up the wall.

I was in one hell of a mess.

Then—when the self-pity threatened to choke me—I forced it aside; forced myself to remember what I *had*. A daughter; a child any man could be proud of, and married to one of the few men who deserved her. I had a television set; a rectangular hole, through which I could watch the outside world and, because of it, be a part of that world. I had a radio; the sounds of the world, the discussions of the world, and some of the music of the world. I had a cassette-player and a good selection of cassettes; the music I'd chosen, and the music I loved, and mine to listen to, any time I felt like it.

These things I had, and for these things I was grateful. Hell knows to *whom* I was grateful ... I was just grateful.

No man can have everything. That's what I told myself ... that no man can have everything.

I had a fine daughter. I had a fine son-in-law. I'd known the love of a fine woman. All these things ... they were enough. I had friends—okay, I had friends—and I was going to sacrifice those friends, and lose them. I was going to be instrumental in putting Collins and Raff behind bars; and, because I would do it, I would also lose the friendship of Dick Sullivan. Three at a swipe! If you *have* to lose friends, don't mess about ... think big.

But, whose bloody fault was it?

Mine?

Like hell it was my fault.

It was David Raff's fault for going crazy on the night of Collins's party; for not keeping his backside anchored to its seat; for thinking he was bigger—that his feelings were more important—than a whole roomful of coppers; for letting murder run riot in his mind, and trying to throw a scare into Paul Gunter. It was Raff's fault.

It was Dick Sullivan's fault, for mouthing stupidities about

136

'vengeance' and things the force couldn't do; for standing there, and deliberately planting the seeds of a rotten weed into fertile ground; for knowing—and, damn it, he *must* have known!—that some lunatic in that assembly would take his words at face value. It was Sullivan's fault.

It was Paulette Fixby's fault, for being weak; for not being a copper's wife, in the real sense of that term; for not accepting the possibility—even the probability—that her man might have to take a swing of the biggest hammer of all; for letting Gunter drive her over the cliff and into self-destruction and, by her self-destruction, underlining—emphasising—the mock-reality of Sullivan's big-mouthed yap. It was Paulette Fixby's fault.

It was Henry Collins's fault, for not being *himself*; for not using that grey stuff he kept under his skull; for being as crazy as Raff and, with Raff, wanting to play 'Avenger', and without a hope in hell of ever pulling it off; for being a bloody fool—all right, *all right*!—and, by being a bloody fool, trusting *me* ... the one man get-at-able by Paul Gunter, because I was the one man who wanted something Collins, and Sullivan, and Raff already had. Legs. It was Collins's fault because, with all his intelligence, he hadn't realised that I (more easily than most men) was capable of being corrupted.

And, because of these fools, I was being made to play cross, and double-cross, and even double-double-cross until I couldn't think straight. Until I drank myself unconscious, ended with a foot stuck behind the central heating pipes, and had to smash it free with a buffet. Until I forgot first principles, and used the bloody foot when it shouldn't have been used. Until, now, there was Christ-only-knew-what wrong with the foot ... and maybe all this twisting and turning had been for nothing ... and maybe gangrene was already in my blood-stream ... and maybe, after all this, I was going to ...

I told myself to clamp down the lid, and I *made* myself clamp down the lid.

I had books, and I had music.

I also (or so I told myself) had patience ... all the patience I needed.

So, screw everything, and I'd sweat it out.

That was on the Friday—Friday afternoon, after Sullivan had been, and gone—and, after that, came the longest hours of my life.

Friday—what remained of Friday—was bearable. Boring, but bearable. I finished Hemingway, and started Uris. Leon Uris ... like most American writers, Uris didn't think he'd written anything worth reading until he had a book at least twice as thick as the same book written by an Englishman. The modern U.S. writers believe in giving at least *weight* for money. Some also gave value, and Uris was one of them.

Again, Collins had introduced us. That first book *Exodus* had been an eye-opener; Collins had dumped it (along with some magazines and a couple of other volumes) on the hospital bedside table. He hadn't said anything (come to think of it, he never *had* said anything—about *anything*—he'd just quietly brought things to my notice, and left the actual discovery to me) and I'd 'discovered' Uris.

And, from the moment I'd closed *Exodus*, Israel had one more champion and Uris had had one more fan.

I'd already enjoyed *Mila 18* and *Battle Cry* and now *Armageddon* was going to make my weekend fly past, without a thought ... at least, that's what I expected.

It didn't.

It wasn't *Armageddon*'s fault. Uris was as good as ever. But who the *hell* can read any book—who the hell can concentrate enough to enjoy good prose—while one part of his mind meanders off along tributaries of thought which have nothing at all to do with the printed words his eyes are reading?

They tell me (rightly, or wrongly) that Napoleon Bonaparte could handle three dispatches at the same time—read one, write one and dictate one ... but I am not Napoleon Bonaparte.

By mid-evening I'd reached the stage where I was turning pages, without knowing a damn what I'd read.

I put the book down, hauled the wheelchair from its hiding place, wormed my way into it, from the armchair, and rolled myself into the kitchen to make a meal.

What sort of a meal?

Hell ... I didn't feel like eating. I didn't need food. I needed what I couldn't get; somebody who knew what he was talking about, to tell me everything was going to be okay.

But, I had to *have* food. My body needed food; if it was going to fight for me it needed nourishment.

I settled for a boiled egg and toast-fingers. I made the meal, and ate it ... and that killed all of thirty minutes!

I checked the T.V. programmes. Nothing. A so-called 'golden-oldie' of the big screen; a crummy film I'd seen, years before, and hadn't even liked then. A re-run (or was it a re-run of a re-run) of a particularly unspectacular 'Spectacular'; a mix some blue-eyed, backroom goon had thought up, with an eye on possible world markets; a glorified montage of chorus girls swinging their tits and waving their arses at the cameras, in the sacred name of 'entertainment'. A 'documentary'; one more re-run, this time of some miserable bastard's way of life—a way of life which wasn't of much interest to him ... and of damn-all interest to anybody else.

For the umpteenth time I wondered why the T.V. people saved *all* their crap for the spring and summer months.

I felt like air.

I trundled the wheelchair to the door, opened the door and sat in the hall, watching nature and the empty road which passed the front of the bungalow. I promised myself twenty motor cars ... after twenty motor cars had passed the bungalow, I'd go back to the armchair.

That's what I'd been reduced to. And by mid-evening, of the Friday. Sitting inside the door, counting bloody motor cars ... and I'd had visions of a week of it. Maybe even a *fortnight*!

I took deep breaths of evening air, and told myself to belt up. To take it easy. To live it, hour at a time; one hour ... and the hell with the next. Enough hours, and I'd have saved up a fortnight. That (I told myself) was the sensible way of doing it ... the only way.

It took longer than the first hour for the twenty bloody cars to pass and, by that time, I was chilling and wishing I'd watched the gyrations of half-dressed chorus girls.

I closed the door, wheeled myself back to the living room, and tossed a mental coin. Leon Uris, or some cassettes?

The cassettes won.

I did all my Gilbert and Sullivans. *The Gondoliers, The Mikado, Pinafore, Iolanthe, The Pirates of Penzance, Ruddigore* and *Yeomen of the Guard.*

I did them all, and it was a mistake. It was three o'clock in the morning before they were finished, and I'd made myself a gigantic meal of indigestible memories ... which was the mistake. Taken a little at a time, I might have enjoyed them (I *would* have enjoyed them) and the sweetness would have masked any bitterness. But too much was too much, and the bitterness worked its way to the surface, and scummed the memories with hurt ... and that was the mistake.

In the early hours (as the first grey of dawn smudged the cloud-wrack, beyond the windows of the kitchen) and as the first birds sent a tentative chirping into a new day, I brewed myself more brandy-laced tea. I wheeled myself back to the living room, dragged myself from the wheelchair to the armchair, then swallowed four Sodium Amytal capsules with the tea ... and didn't give grain-sized damn whether, or not, I was going to wake up.

I went out like a blackjack had landed at the base of my skull.

It was well into Saturday, before I saw the world again.

Well into Saturday—almost mid-day ... and the telephone bell was ringing like the clappers.

It was Susan.

She said, 'Hello, pop. Were you in bed?'

'Bed?' I muttered. (I struggled to tear the curtain of cobwebs away from my brain.)

'It's been ringing a long time.'

'Oh!'

'Sorry if I've got you out of bed.'

'No—it's—er ... y'know. A bit of a lie-in. That's all. I—er—I had a late night.'

She gave a quick laugh, and said, 'On the tiles, I hope.'

'Eh? No—oh, no ... not quite.' I made a noise which, I hoped, would reach her ears as a counter-laugh. 'Berlin, actually.'

'*Where?*'

'The Leon Uris book. *Armageddon*. It was three, before I could put it down.'

'A good book?'

'A good book,' I agreed.

She said, 'Sorry I didn't ring, last night.'

'Eh?' (For Christ's sake, I hadn't noticed! I'd been so brim-filled with once-upon-a-time thoughts I hadn't even noticed *that*.)

I said, 'That's—er—that's okay, honey. You—er—you can't ...'

'Chris got some tickets.'

'What?'

'A couple of spare tickets ... somebody had booked, and couldn't get, at the last minute. Leeds. The D'Oyly Carte ...'

Somebody whispered, 'Oh, my God!' and it must have been me.

'What's that, pop?'

'Nothing. Nothing, honey. You were saying?'

'It was *Yeomen* ... y'know, *The Yeomen of the Guard*.

'You—er—you liked it?' I asked, hoarsely.

'Of course. I cried.'

'Oh!'

'It's not like the others, is it, pop? Y'know ... not comic?'

'No ... not like the others,' I agreed.

'Jack Point. He's an awfully sad character.'

'Aye.'

'Anyway, I'll tell you about it, this afternoon.'

'What?' I shoved daggers of concentration into my mind.

'This afternoon. Chris finishes at two, and we thought we'd have a run out, to see ...'

'No!' I cut in. 'Don't—y'know ... don't do that.'

I could almost see the tiny frown of puzzlement, as she said, 'Sorry, pop. I don't see what you ...'

'I'm going out,' I blurted. 'All weekend. This afternoon, until Monday.'

'Oh!'

'Henry's going to ...'

'Mr Collins?'

'Aye. He's going to pick me up. We're—er—spending the weekend, together.'

'Oh!'

I said, 'Look, honey—I hope you're not too disappointed. It's just that ...'

'Pop,' she said, 'is there anything wrong?'

'Wrong?' I tried to put amazement into the return-question.

'You sound ... funny.'

'Funny?'

'Odd.'

'Honey—I've just crawled from bed. I'm still bog-eyed. Maybe I *sound* bog-eyed.'

'You'd tell me,' she said, sombrely.

'What?' I kidded not to understand.

'If anything was wrong ... you'd tell me.'

'There's nothing wrong. Where the hell d'you get the idea that ...'

'You'd *tell* me,' she insisted.

'Who else?' I fenced.

'Just—y'know ... if not, I'd be awfully hurt.'

'I know, honey.' I sighed, then said, 'Believe me. I'd tell you.'

'Okay.' She sounded convinced ... almost convinced. Then she said, 'Have a nice weekend, pop.'

'What?'

'With Mr Collins. Enjoy yourself.'

'Oh—ah ... aye. It'll be nice. He's good company.'

'I'll ring you Monday. Monday night. Okay?'

'That'll be fine.'

''Bye, pop. God bless.'

She hung up.

I whispered, 'God bless,' into the dead mouthpiece.

In the bathroom, I looked at the foot. It had grown to be that. 'The foot'—not 'my foot' ... it was another exercise in self-deception. I wanted no part of the bloody thing. I disowned it. It wasn't mine. It wasn't even a foot any more—not what is meant by the word 'foot'—instead, it was ... Christ only knew *what* it was!

Puffed and multi-coloured, with green and yellow pus weeping from the torn flesh. A mockery of a foot. A Frankensteinian foot. A shapeless blob of putrefying muck, stuck at the end of a dead leg.

I stared at it.

I whispered, 'Oh, my Christ ... *no!*'

And that, too, was one more tiny piece of personal kidology. I knew damn well that it was 'yes'.

I washed the monstrosity, doused it in antiseptic, then covered it with the seaboot stocking . Nothing else. Just something to hide it from sight ... and, after that, the hell with it!

Back in the living room, I wheeled around and opened all the windows and all the doors. Including the front door of the bungalow. The place stank like a Peruvian knocking-shop; old tobacco smoke, the sour smell of the previous night, and something else. A faint, sickly-sweet stench. Not strong—not over-powering—but *there* ... and I conned myself into believing I didn't know what it was.

Into the kitchen, for a meal.

I had to eat. Common sense—simple gumption—insisted that I must eat; nourishment was vital, if ... if ...

Christ Almighty, I *had* to eat!

Eggs?

Who the blazes wants eggs, at a time like this? Who the hell wants to mess around frying eggs? Boiling eggs? Scrambling eggs? Who the hell wants *eggs*?

Okay, if not eggs, bacon?

Bacon? Dead flesh? Some dead pig (something like myself), cured, sliced, then sizzled in hot fat? What is this? ... some sort of sick joke?

Bread?

Bread? What is it? ... the 'staff of life'? At a time like this? Life?

Life!

LIFE!!

I came out of it sweating. I came out of it with a rush. I came out of it gripping the arms of the wheelchair so tightly—so fiercely —that the muscles of my fingers and of my wrists screamed silent protest.

I came out of it with clenched teeth, and talking ... almost shouting.

'Knock it off, Ripley. Knock it *off*! What the flaming hell d'you want? ... immortality?'

Then I came out of it.

I was trembling a little and, when I raised my hand and wiped my face, the palm came away wet with perspiration. I took a few deep breaths, wiped some more sweat from my face, then told some of the truth. I talked to myself ... as if I was two people; one a terrified fool, and the other a man capable of accepting the inevitable.

I said, 'Ease up, boy. You don't know ... you don't yet know, for sure. Maybe. Maybe not. They have antibiotics, these days. They can handle these things. Ease it over the weekend ... that's all. Then ... We-ell, if they can't—they *can't* ... period.'

Then I forced myself to forget it.

I wasn't being brave. Don't get any weird ideas. I was scared. I was scared stupid, whenever I probed possibilities. So, I didn't probe possibilities ... and it was as easy as that. I dropped a mental curtain, and refused to allow myself even so much as a peek beyond its fringe.

I could do it, because I hadn't feeling—I hadn't the ever-present reminder of pain—therefore the curtain could only be torn aside by will-power. It was a reversal ... get it? It was a blessing. With feeling, the will-power would have had to be used to ignore the pain, and to keep the curtain closed. Without feeling, there was no pain and the will-power was necessary to *remember* what was at the bottom of my leg.

I dropped the curtain, and turned my back on it.

I filled the electric kettle, plugged it in and, while it boiled, I trundled into the bathroom, sluiced my hands and face and ran an electric razor over my cheeks.

I had buttered toast and marmalade and, contrary to what I'd expected, I enjoyed it. There was a taste about it I hadn't, previously, noticed; a taste which, to that time, I'd taken for granted. Toast and marmalade—it had a taste ... so what? But, suddenly, the tangy bite of the lemon marmalade was mouth-cleansing and a minor toothsome experience. And the bread; cut thick, and lightly toasted to a faint bronze; crisp-skinned, but soft-centred, and soaked in melted butter. And the tea; strong and sweet and lightened by condensed milk; 'Sergeant Major Special'; good and hot, and sipped slowly from a heavy beaker.

That meal, simple though it was, had a taste I'd previously missed.

Beautiful, and sharp-edged ... like a culinary camera which, until that moment, had been slightly out of focus but which had now been righted.

After the meal, I washed the crockery and the knife and spoon; and the hot water from the kitchen tap seemed to sooth my hands, and the suds of the washing-up liquid caressed my fingers, and the tea-towel was soft, like lamb's wool, to my touch, and even the curves of the beaker, and the plate, and the spoon and the knife-handle had a beauty and symmetry I hadn't previously noticed.

I stacked the beaker and the plate on their shelf—returned the knife and spoon to their drawer—and I performed these simple tasks deliberately and with precision. Then back, again to the bathroom, to enjoy what Elaine had called 'a stand-up bath'.

In the early days; when we'd first set up home together; when bobbies lived in houses other people didn't want. When a bathroom, in a police house, was a luxury and not (as now) taken for granted.

We'd used the kitchen and, each evening (before going to bed) we'd stripped, kept carefully to within the confines of a folded towel and washed ourselves, from top to toe ... 'a stand-up bath'.

We'd laughed at this stupid inconvenience and, to us, it had never been an inconvenience. It had been one of the highlights of the day. A silly little adventure. A private joke, which was exclusively 'ours'.

There had been no inhibitions. No modesty. No shame—what the hell had we to be ashamed of? ... we both had good bodies, and each body had belonged as much to the one of us as to the other. It had been part of early marriage.

A laughing, happy, soap-sudded, water-splashing, towelling-down romp ... 'a stand-up bath'. So much part of our life that, when we *had* progressed to a house with the super-luxury of a bathroom, we'd still bathed together; sharing the tub and wallowing around like healthy young seals each playing tag with the other's soap-slippery body.

I had 'a stand-up bath' ... and felt a twinge of regret that Elaine wasn't there, as in the old days, to scrub my back.

(And this, too—in retrospect—was part of the huge con-trick. It wasn't 'a stand-up bath' ... not really. It was, I suppose, 'a sit-down bath'. A shuffling from the wheelchair and onto the cork-seated bathroom chair. And, after that 'a sit-down bath'. But I kidded myself. It was as near as I could get. It was, as far as *I* was concerned, 'a stand-up bath' and, had she been there, Elaine would have understood and, perhaps, have been pleased that I remembered.)

I dried myself, tumbled back into the wheelchair, naked, and wheeled myself into the bedroom. I put on clean pyjamas. I put a new seaboot stocking on 'the foot'. I made 'the foot' a thing which might not force the world to spew its disgust; I hid its hideousness beneath freshly laundered wool.

Then I struggled into a dressing-gown and steered myself into the living room.

Fresh air had cleared away the stench.

The cassettes were scattered on the table, around the radio-cum-cassette-player and, for a moment, a sharp needle of the previous night's agony touched my memory ... but I snapped it off, before its point could inject more of the old poison.

I collected the cassettes and began to slip them into their respective plastic packs and, as I was performing this simple cleaning-up task, a thought struck me.

A great thought. A wonderful thought.

What I needed—I suddenly realised it—was, not quite companionship, but somebody to whom I could talk. Not a listener, exactly; a listener might listen ... and just that. He (she) might not *hear*. Might not understand ... might not even *try* to understand.

He (she) might even interrupt. Might question. Might become bored with what I was trying to say.

And yet ...

Confession (or so they say) is good for the soul. Some of the most profound thinkers (or so I'm told) arrive at their most profound conclusions via talking aloud; they have the gift of talking and, at the same time, listening.

I knew I hadn't that gift.

But I had the mechanical equivalent of that gift.

147

I had a cassette-player. I had casettes ... scores of cassettes. And (somewhere in the bedroom) I had a microphone. I knew enough about the workings of the cassette-player to know that, when the microphone was plugged in, the machine did two things simultaneously; it wiped the tape clean of whatever was already on the tape and, at the same time, recorded whatever the microphone was picking up.

So-o ...

Talk. Then listen. Then, talk again. Then, listen again.

Eventually, some sort of sense had to come out of it ... if only the sense of a man who doesn't know what the hell he was talking about.

I was suddenly very excited.

It was as if I'd suddenly stumbled across the long-lost secret of immortality.

I returned to the bedroom, rummaged around in the back of the wardrobe, found the box, in which the radio-cum-cassette-player had been bought, and found the microphone.

I returned to the living room, and sorted through the cassettes.

So many—more than fifty—and, to tell the truth, I didn't want to ruin any of them. The Gilbert and Sullivans—they were out ... definitely *out*! The same with the Mozarts and the Tchaikovskys; to wipe them, would be a little like murdering a well-loved friend. I sorted through them. Those I loved, and those I merely 'liked' ... not because they were less beautiful, but because their beauty (or much of their beauty) escaped me, because of my own lack of true appreciation.

Eventually, I chose my sacrificial victims. Bruckner's third symphony. Cello concertoes by Haydn, Boccherini and Vivaldi, a couple of Nielsen symphonies and some Scarlatti sonatas. I was (I knew) committing what some people would look upon as artistic vandalism, but a choice had to be made ... and I made it.

I rigged up the microphone and the cassette-player, slipped a cassette into the slot, switched on and tried a run-through.

I recited *Mary Mary Quite Contrary* into the microphone, switched to back-wind, then played my own voice back to myself. As usual (and as with everybody) I was mildly surprised at the sound of my own voice; it was at least half an octave lower than I thought it was, and smeared with the broad vowels of Yorkshire ... not that I was ashamed of my origin but, had you asked, I'd have taken an oath that I'd long ago smoothed the dialect out of my speech.

However ...

It seemed okay. Maybe the microphone should be a little nearer. Maybe I should forget the microphone, and just chat—as to a friend—and see what the hell came out.

I switched the cassette-player to 'record', trailed the wires of the set and the microphone across the room, hoisted myself from the wheelchair and into the armchair, re-positioned the microphone, switched on, leaned back, clasped my hands across my stomach, closed my eyes and started talking.

'He's been nobbled,' said Sullivan, grimly.

'It would,' observed Collins, gently, 'take a good man to—er—nobble Charles Ripley.'

In a flat voice, which carried absolute conviction, Sullivan repeated, 'He's been nobbled.'

Collins strolled to the hi-fi set-up, touched a switch, and the soft tinkle of a Bach Harpsichord Concerto stopped half-way through a phrase.

Collins strolled back towards the wing-chairs, and said, 'A delightful present.'

'What?' Sullivan frowned.

'The records ... a delightful present. To be treasured, rest assured.'

'Oh! ... that?'

'Sherry?' offered Collins, politely.

'No ... no, thanks.'

'A cigarette?' Collins motioned a hand towards the sandalwood-and-ivory cigarette box on the military-chest coffee-table.

'Thanks ... no.' Sullivan sounded irritable. Impatient. He said, 'Look—I don't know what the hell's happened—but ...'

'I know. You suspect Charles of having been approached by the opposition and, presumably, accepting a bribe.' Collins lowered himself into the companion wing-chair to that being used by Sullivan, smiled, and murmured, 'What a ridiculous idea.'

'He changed his story,' growled Sullivan.

'Surely not.'

'He told the copper at Harrogate a straightforward yarn, then told me a tarted-up version of it.'

'An "amplification", perhaps?' suggested Collins, mildly.

'A big enough "amplification" to make it a complete waste of time taking the bloody thing to court.'

'In which case,' said Collins, solemnly, 'it was always just that ... a waste of time taking it to court.'

'A man has his pocket picked. He was ...'

'As I understand it,' interrupted Collins, gently. Musingly. 'All this excitement has been generated because a stupid man deserved to have his pocket picked ... and, possibly did have his pocket picked. On the other hand, there is an equal possibility that this stupid man's wallet fell out of his pocket. Either way, a trivial thing. Certainly not worthy of the attention of an Assistant Chief Constable (Crime). Which, in turn, prompts the question ... why?'

'Why, what?' asked Sullivan.

'Why are you suddenly interested in trivia, Richard?' Collins smiled, good-naturedly.

'There's no such thing as "trivial" crime,' said Sullivan gruffly.

'Not when you're lecturing the members of some Women's Institute,' agreed Collins. 'But—forgive me—at the moment you're talking to a man who has had to place certain practical priorities upon certain types of crime ... and who knows that the theft of a milk bottle is most certainly not as "untrivial" as a murder.'

Sullivan grunted, bad-temperedly.

'Which,' drawled Collins, 'prompts my question ... why? Why does an A.C.C.(Crime) concern himself with an unimportant case of theft from the person? And, what is more, one which wasn't even committed in his own police area?'

Sullivan said, 'Stop being long-winded, Henry. Stop asking questions you know the answers to.'

'Charles?' Collins raised a well-bred eyebrow.

'And Gunter?'

Collins looked surprised, then said, 'Ah, now there you have me, Richard. Why Gunter?'

'It's a sort of freemasonry ... you know that.'

'Criminals?'

'They scratch each others backs,' growled Sullivan.

'And?'

'Damn it all, why should he?' Sullivan mixed anger, disgust and worry in his tone. 'Charlie Ripley isn't bent ... anything but. And—to the best of my knowledge—Gunter hasn't much say in Harrogate. But there's a connection. I'm bloody sure there is.'

'Gut bobbying?' There was suave mockery in the question.

'Don't knock it,' growled Sullivan. 'It's solved more crime than all the test tubes in the world.'

'It presupposes that Gunter has some sort of hold over Charles.'

'Look.' Blunt—almost rude—concern etched near-ugliness across Sullivan's expression as he looked into Collins's face. 'You and Raff tried to talk Charlie Ripley into this lunatic idea of yours. To kill Gunter. He almost fell for it. I'm not so bloody blind—I could see that ... he almost fell for it. I told him—all right, I admit it—I told him to get back amongst you. To get to know what cockeyed scheme you might have thought up. Then report back to me. He couldn't—he admitted that to me, yesterday ... that you wouldn't wear it. That's the real reason I went to see him. To ask him. And now this ... a change of story. There's a connection. Somewhere. Don't ask me how I know, or what the connection is. But it's there ... gut bobbying, if you like. Gunter and Ripley. There's a link. And—damn you, for a cunning old devil, Henry Collins—you're in it, somewhere. It's a puzzler, and it's worrying me, and I want to know what the hell's going on.'

Collins opened the cigarette box. He chose a cigarette, fitted the cigarette into a briar holder, flicked the table-lighter into flame and kissed the flame with the tip of the holdered cigarette. His habitual ploy, whenever he was choosing his words carefully; seeming to give far more attention to the simple movements of his hands than he was giving to the words.

He drawled, 'I must warn you, Richard. Gunter is still under sentence of death. Very much so. David Raff is as keen as ever. So am I. We think we can do it, and get away with it. We think we can do it, and leave insufficient proof of our participation ... and this, despite the fact that you know in advance. It is a certain —shall we say—vanity, on our part. We expect you to do your best ... naturally. But we're quite sure your best won't be good enough.

'Now—as to your basic question ... why has Charles changed his story regarding the pickpocket? I confess, it puzzles me a little. I can only assume that you, yourself, have arrived at the correct conclusion. That Gunter has friends in Harrogate, and that Charles is modifying his original statement as a favour to Gunter. Which—I agree—suggests that Gunter holds some sort of threat over Charles. A threat—or, perhaps, a promise. A bribe, perhaps?'

'Charlie Ripley wouldn't take a backhander,' growled Sullivan.

'There is,' murmured Collins, 'an adage which suggests that every man has his price.'

'Charlie Ripley would not take a backhander,' repeated Sullivan.

Collins moved his shoulders.

Sullivan hesitated, sighed, then said, 'See him ... eh?'

'I beg your pardon?'

'He's a mate of yours,' muttered Sullivan. 'He's a mate of mine, too ... but I'm still a copper. You're not. He might open up to you. If he does, let me know ... as a favour.'

'You really are an amazing person, Richard,' chuckled Collins.

'Eh ... why?'

'We-ell, now ... First you ask Charles to spy on me. Now you ask me to spy on Charles. The situation has certain humorous overtones ... don't you think?'

'No ... I'm damned if I do.'

'From where we stand, I mean.'

'Henry,' Sullivan spoke sombrely. Grimly, and with a certain *pleading quality in his voice. 'Just for a change—just for a pleasant change—forget where you stand, and look at the thing from where I stand. I'm the top jack in this force. I haven't too many friends ... popularity doesn't go with the job. But I have three. Charlie Ripley, David Raff and Henry Collins. I like 'em —all three of 'em ... I like 'em a lot. And, between 'em, they're giving me nightmares. They're like kids released from a boarding-school ... they're running wild. They're playing ducks and drakes with the criminal law ... that, or they have visions of doing. And, when they come unstuck—and, sure as hell they will come un-stuck—it'll be my job to slap 'em inside. I shall not enjoy the job, Henry. Believe me ... I shall not enjoy it. But I'll bloody-well do it!'*

'Of course,' murmured Collins.

'But, if playing both ends against the middle can save me that job, I'll do that, too,' continued Sullivan. 'I'll have 'em chasing each others tails till they're dizzy ... if it uses up their energy, and keeps 'em out of trouble. Do I make myself clear?'

'Oh yes ... quite clear.'

'So?'

'You have,' smiled Collins, 'a very soft centre, Richard. You're not half as hard as you pretend to be ... you never were.'

'For the Lord Harry's sake!'

'Give me a reason,' said Collins, gently.

'Eh?'

'For visiting Charles. For suddenly showing up on his door-step. Give me a reason he'll accept, without being suspicious.'

'Oh! ... er—ah.' Sullivan snapped his fingers. 'Tell him you've called to enquire about his ankle.'

'His ankle?' Collins stopped smiling.

'He's sprained his ankle ... twisted it, I think. Tell him you bumped into me, and that I mentioned it. That you've—y'know ... called to see if there's anything he needs. If you can help ... that sort of thing.'

'It's—er—it's a little more serious than that, Richard.' Collins frowned.

'Serious?' Collins's concern was caught, but not yet understood, by Sullivan.

'Charles,' explained Collins. 'This business of being paralysed from the waist. It means a very bad blood supply. Poor circulation ... very poor circulation indeed.'

'Aye. I—er—I suppose,' muttered Sullivan.

'Charles ... He knows it—I'm sure he must have been told ... but he won't accept it.'

Sullivan growled, 'He's pig-headed.'

'Heavens above, you're both pig-headed,' snapped Collins, angrily. 'I'd hate to have to put my finger on either of you and say that one was more stupidly pig-headed than the other. But, at least, you're healthy. With Charles, the least injury below the waist—something you, or I, might shrug off—and it becomes serious. Very quickly. The blood doesn't carry the poison away. Anything can happen.'

'He hasn't seen a doctor,' muttered Sullivan. And the worry was there in total, now. And the concerned misery.

'The fool!' Collins stood up from his chair and squashed what was left of his cigarette into the ash-tray.

'You're—er—you're going to see him.'

Collins said, 'Yes—I'm going to see him. And now—as a favour to me—stop wasting your time worrying about pickpockets. Concentrate on more important things. Gunter, for example. And, if not Gunter, Charles. He's supposed to be your friend ... remember?'

Sullivan looked miserable.

He'd deserved the rebuke, and he couldn't remember when he'd seen Collins so obviously angry.

I'm sorry about Raff. All the way through, I've talked about Raff as if he was near-certifiable. He isn't ... obviously he isn't. He's a good man. A decent man. He was once a good copper. Never great—but he'd be the first to agree that few coppers are that, and that he wasn't one of them ... but, nevertheless, good. When he reigned the city C.I.D. he held the cork down on some very explosive situations. He and I worked on some good cases. Including a few murder enquiries. He was reliable ... bloody reliable!

Which, in coppering, means everything. Give me a reliable copper who's run-of-the-mill to a genius who can't be trusted, every time. You know where you stand ... *exactly* where you stand. And you know your back's guarded, which means a lot.

David Raff has guarded a few backs in his time. Including mine. So, don't get the wrong idea about David Raff. They don't come better.

I'm only sorry that, last Monday night, at Collins's party, I asked the wrong question of his wife. I didn't mean it to be wrong. If Elaine had been there, it wouldn't have been wrong ... because it wouldn't have been asked.

It was a damn-fool question, asked by a thoughtless oaf, and it touched one of David's sensitive areas. It upset him, and before Gunter did his Daniel-in-the-lion's-den act and, if I hadn't asked the question, it is possible that the Raff-Gunter face-out wouldn't have happened. It is possible that David might have hung onto his temper ... and that all this might not have happened.

All this is might-have-been talk ... but it is, at least, possible.

Like most men, I unconsciously use other men's weaknesses as an excuse for my own shortcomings. I think I've done so, with Raff.

If I have, I'm sorry.

It was late-afternoon—crawling towards evening—and I suddenly felt the pangs of hunger. Good, old-fashioned hunger. I was (to use an expression from my home county) 'clammed'. I could have eaten a nag-sandwich ... a horse, between two haystacks.

It was a nice feeling. It made a happy change from shoving food into the hole in my face, merely for the sake of stoking up the boiler.

I also figured it was time I listened to some decent music.

Mozart's 'Fortieth'.

Okay ... musically, I'm a complete square. Some of the pieces Henry Collins raves about leave me cold. Conversely, some of the things I like, *he's* introduced me to. But, what I don't understand I don't enjoy and (I don't give a damn how clever it is) if I don't enjoy it I count it a waste of time listening.

Mozart ... now, there is a character who talks *my* language.

I'd known Mozart a long, long time. As long as I could remember. The *Eine Kleine Nachtmusik. Don Giovanni. The Marriage of Figaro.* The 'famous three' ... the 'thirty-ninth', the 'fortieth' and the 'forty-first'.

It was one of the things (one of the thousand things) which made our marriage gell. That we liked—okay, *loved*—music from the same mould; that, when we called a piece 'our' piece, it became just that ... something we could listen to, and enjoy, every day. And I mean that. *Every* day. We never tired of it. I know (Henry has, in the past, smilingly teased Elaine ... and me) by the wider definition of the term 'music lover' we were both stilted people; we refused to 'experiment'; we were conservative ... with a small 'c'. Okay—that's what we were ... that's what I still am. Who cares, as long as I enjoy the music I like.

I like Mozart's 'Fortieth' ... which is why I fixed the cassette-player to give me Mozart's 'Fortieth' while I made a meal.

Pancakes.

I suddenly felt a yearning for pancakes; thin enough to be almost transparent. Stacked, one on top of the other and, sandwiched between each pancake, a layer of hot, golden syrup.

Jesus! ... my mouth almost salived at the thought.

In retrospect, I can see that I was happy. Christ on His throne knows *why* I was happy; things hadn't altered—the triggers of the anger and the frustrations of the last few days were still there. I was still wheeling 'the foot' around. Paul Gunter still had me nailed to the floor. I was still going to do the dirt on two of my best friends. Everything!

Nothing had changed ... I was just happy.

Maybe talking some of it out had done something. Maybe just listening to it being told back to me, as if it was some sort of fiction which hadn't really happened, had shooed the spiders of disgust back into the corners of their webs.

Maybe ...

Whatever the reason, I was happy.

I made the pancakes, warmed the syrup, listened to Mozart and could have the luxury of memories without hurt.

I was eating the last of the pancakes when Collins arrived.

Henry looked worried. Relaxed ... but worried. His face was a few shades paler than usual, and his eyes had that slightly vague, far-away look of a man with things on his mind.

He rang the bell, and I called him inside, from the kitchen.

As he entered I wheeled my tray to the sink, ran hot water, added washing-up liquid and played at being the-busy-little-housewife. As we exchanged the first pleasantries, Henry took a clean tea-towel from its rack and, as I washed the dishes and cutlery, he dried. It must have looked pretty funny; a cripple in a wheelchair washing-up, and an elegantly turned out middle-aged man doing the drying.

It didn't feel funny ... it felt friendly.

'I saw Richard, today,' he said, off-handedly.

'Uhu?'

'He said you'd hurt your foot. Twisted your ankle.'

I said, 'It's nothing much. Y'know ... I was clumsy.'

'I see.' He stacked the crockery, neatly, as he dried it; placed the cutlery in its drawer.

I said, 'He was a bit peeved.'

'Peeved?' His expression said he didn't understand.

'I saw a pickpocket at work. Thursday—at Harrogate ... at the Yorkshire match. Dick came for a statement. It wasn't quite what he wanted.'

'No?'

'There was—y'know ... an element of doubt.'

'That there *hadn't* been a theft?'

'It's possible,' I said. 'Just possible ... that the wallet had slipped from the man's pocket, and that the thief had picked it up from the ground.'

'Oh ... I see.'

'Dick didn't like me saying so.'

Collins murmured, 'No ... he wouldn't. It gives the thief a loophole.'

'Aye.' I pulled the plug from the sink and, quietly, and on an impulse, said, 'He didn't, of course.'

'What?'

'Pick it up from the ground. He stole it, from the man's pocket.'

'Oh!' He folded the towel and returned it to its rack. He began, 'In that case, why not ...'

'Gunter wants a favour,' I growled.

'I *see.*'

Without being asked—without making it seem like a favour, and without even making me feel like a cripple—he took the handles of the wheelchair and steered me into the living room.

He said, 'Richard mentioned it ... in passing. That you'd arrested a petty criminal. You're to be congratulated, Charles.'

'Think so?' I grinned, a little ruefully. 'Dick might not agree.'

'Richard doesn't *know* everything ... does he?' he said, gently.

'Not by a country mile.'

The Mozart ended with its string section flourish.

'Anything else?' asked Collins.

'No ... let's talk.'

'I'd like that,' murmured Collins. He walked to the cassette-player, pressed the 'Off' switch, then settled into an armchair. He said, 'What shall we talk about? Your foot?'

'It's not important. Just a twisted ankle.'

'Is that all?' The question called me a liar, in the nicest possible way.

'Look—it's ...'

'Charles—forgive me—but I can smell it from here.'

'Oh!'

'I want to help,' he said, quietly. 'Let me look at it.'

'Don't bother,' I said, gruffly. 'It's mangled to hell and back.'

'Therefore, you should see a doctor.'

'No!'

'Charles.' He was suddenly very serious. Very concerned. 'Anything wrong in the part that's paralysed, and ...'

'I know,' I growled.

'If mortification sets in ...'

'A polite name for gangrene.' I smiled. It wasn't a humorous smile. Nor, come to that, was it a non-humorous smile. It was just

158

a smile ... and pretty meaningless. I said, 'It's already there ...
that's what you can smell.'

'I'm very sorry,' he said, gently.

'Don't be ... I'm not.'

His expression asked a question.

'Oh, I *was*.' I shrugged an unconcern which I didn't wholly
feel. I said, 'Believe me, I've done some wallowing in self-pity,
these last few days. But—what the hell! ... it's not painful. I
can't feel a damn thing.'

'Nevertheless ...' he began.

'No doctor,' I interrupted. 'A doctor means amputation ...
or, bloody lucky, if not. What I have is no use to me, but I'm
damned if I'm having *less*.'

He began to perform his cigarette-lighting routine. I'd expected
it ... with a man like Henry Collins, few things are really pre-
dictable, but those that are, *really* are. Where other men needed a
stiff whisky—or maybe even to *smoke* a cigarette—Collins needed
the carefully calculated movements of his fingers; the choosing
of the cigarette, the fitting it into the holder ... slow, and fiddling
movements but, to him, very necessary.

As he worked, he talked. And I answered his oblique questions.
He said, 'You miss her, Charles.'

'Hell's bells.' I shook my head. 'You'll never know.'

'You're a lucky man ... I don't have to tell you.'

'You don't have to tell me.'

'There are marriages ... and marriages.'

'Only one, like that. Only one in a lifetime ... in a hundred
lifetimes.'

'Susan?'

'She has Chris. With luck there'll be a repeat performance.'

'Quite. I'm sure.'

'Aye—me, too ... *I'm* sure.'

'Does—er—does Richard know?'

'No.'

'No ... I thought not. He told me it was a sprained ankle.'

'That's what I told *him*. He didn't press ... I didn't tell him.'

Collins said, 'He has his own problems, of course.'

'Gunter, for example.'

159

'Gunter, for example,' he agreed.

I said, 'Gunter doesn't know, either.'

As he lighted the cigarette, he said, 'Is there any reason why he should?'

'No. Except—y'know ... I'm supposed to be on his pay-roll.'

'Ah! Yes—I'd—er ... I should have remembered, shouldn't I?'

I tried to time it accurately; left a moment or two of silence, before saying what I wanted him to both hear and understand.

Then, I said, 'I'm still with you, Henry.'

His look of surprise almost amounted to shock.

'Why not?' I asked. 'Does this make any difference? *Should* it?'

'Logically,' he said, slowly, 'it shouldn't.'

'Okay ... let's deal in logic.'

There was another piece of silence, this time of his choosing. It stretched into seconds, and I knew he was picking the right words with which to say something which might be hurtful ... but without wanting to hurt. He drew on his cigarette as he pondered.

Then, he said, 'Charles—please be honest—is there any possibility of you changing your mind? ... of you deciding to see a doctor?'

'Not a hope,' I grunted.

'I wish you would. I mean that ... I truly wish you would.'

'Sorry.' I shook my head.

'I think I know the reason,' he said, sadly.

I gave him a half-smile of encouragement, and said, 'It's a good enough reason. A damn good reason ... as far as *I'm* concerned.'

'It seems ...' He ran out of words, and moved his hands, expressively.

'Not insufficient,' I said, softly.

He glanced at my seaboot-stockinged foot, and said, 'There's no easy way of saying it, Charles. You're dying.'

'Dead,' I corrected him.

'Without treatment, it will spread.'

'Painlessly ... as I understand these things.'

'I'm ...' He hesitated, then said, 'I'm not sure ... eventually. I'm no expert.'

'Let's say "painlessly",' I suggested.

'This is a disgusting subject,' he said, heavily. 'It's—it's a very distressing subject. It's like—it's like ...'

'Henry,' I smiled. 'I've been a very lonely man. Too bloody lonely. I'm sorry—don't get me wrong—but you're a born bachelor ... very self-sufficient. However hard you try, you'll never understand. I'm crippled, old son. It isn't just that I can't walk. It isn't just that I have to use irons and crutches. That I could live with ... once. I've tried to live with 'em since. I swear, I've really *tried*. And not just for my sake. For the sake of ... Let's say for the sake of a belief. A belief I was sold—a belief I didn't have, to start off with ... but a belief I was sold. I bought that belief, mate ... and the price was too bloody high! It was a damn sight higher than I'd ever expected. And now, I'm bankrupt. I can't buy any more beliefs. I can't afford 'em. I don't *want* 'em.' I watched his eyes and, very quietly, said, 'I'm dying, Henry. Everybody dies. Now, let's drop the subject ... let's talk about something else.'

'Gunter?'

'Let's talk about Gunter,' I agreed.

We talked about Gunter.

Correction we talked *around* Gunter.

Nothing specific. We agreed that he was beyond the law; that he had enough people tucked away in his pocket to make him virtually inviolate as far as common justice was concerned. That he ran the city—and more than the city—and that, because of this, he was making a laughing-stock of the force.

People knew ... too many people knew.

Decent people were tired—or fast tiring—of bobbies who enforced the Road Traffic Law, but couldn't touch a bastard who lived fat on major crime and corruption. Couldn't touch ... or *wouldn't* touch.

That was the thing that rankled.

The ordinary bloke—the man-in-the-street—figured the force was on the twist. And why not? Who could blame him? He *knew* ... as much as *we* knew. But what he didn't know was that 'knowledge' and 'proof' aren't even horses from the same stable. That there are men walking the streets, today—not just the Gunters of the world, but apparently decent, upright, law-abiding citizens—who are murderers ... that they've killed, and that the coppers know damn well they've killed, and that *they* know the coppers know damn well they've killed. It isn't something they mention at Police Colleges, but it's something every copper with service under his belt gets to know; that that tiny piece of evidence is still missing—that there's a link still needed to complete the chain ... and that, until that link is found, 'knowledge' and 'proof' don't run together.

It's a hard world—a stinking world ... and we agreed upon *that*.

Before he left I rolled the wheelchair to the bureau, tore a sheet from a scribbling pad, wrote on it, folded the sheet and handed it to Collins.

I said, 'In the bedroom. There's a safe ... alongside the wardrobe, and fitted into the wall. It has a dial-lock. That's the number. Nobody else knows it ... just the two of us. Not even Susan. Empty it ... eh? Use your discretion.'

He took the paper, looked uncomfortable, and said, 'Look—Charles—I really think ...'

'As a favour,' I insisted. 'As a friend.'

He sighed, slipped the folded paper into his wallet and returned the wallet to his inside pocket, without saying a word.

I suddenly felt awkward.

I muttered, 'Well—that's it, then ... isn't it?'

'It would seem so,' agreed Collins, quietly.

'Goodbye, Henry. Don't—y'know ... don't worry.'

We shook hands, and he left.

He looked sad. I wished he didn't—there was no reason for his sadness ... but, in his place, I figure I, too, might have felt a little sad.

* * *

I replugged the microphone, slipped another cassette into its slot, filled and lighted a pipe, and did some more thinking aloud.

What I said about crooks and coppers—about power-hunger and mental corruption, about the five-per-cent rackets—the poacher-turned-gamekeeper argument I'd used to build up a smoke-screen, from behind which I'd performed my own involved crossing and double-crossing act ... it was all bullshit.

Of course it was.

The force isn't built that way ... and, if it was, it wouldn't be the best in the world. Okay, you get the odd rogue cop. Come to that, you also get the odd rogue doctor ... rogue solicitor ... rogue accountant. They're around. The world may be a rose-bower, but the thorns come with the blooms ... and the thorns sometimes make people forget the fragrance. It's a nifty way of putting it. Very poetic ... but you know what I mean.

Me?

I've been hooked on a thorn for a few years. Prior to that, I was intoxicated by the perfume; so damn intoxicated that I forgot one of the basic laws of nature ... that everything (but *everything*!) has to be paid for.

Let me tell you, friend. When they work that shroud over your head the scales are dead level; what you've put in, you've got out; what you've given you've *had* given. Every tiny piece of bastardy has been paid for. Every split-second of happiness you've ever been responsible for has been returned.

That which makes a life is a little like energy—it can't be created from nothing, it can't be reduced to nothingness ... it's *there*. You take it, you use it and, when you've finished with it, you pass it on—because it's still *there* ... no bigger, no smaller than it was when you first grabbed it.

I put it badly. I have no fine way with words. What I mean has, no doubt, been said many times, and better. But (right or wrong) it is a comfortable philosophy, and I believe it ... therefore, it comforts me.

I unplugged the microphone and returned it to the bedroom. Whatever else, I didn't want anybody to get suspicious; to see something and, from that something, build up a distrust. A microphone, for example ... a man (a man like Gunter) walks into a room, spots a microphone and immediately jumps to wrong conclusions.

I didn't want that to happen.

I took what I needed from the back of the wardrobe, checked it, made it ready, then took it back into the living room and hid it behind the window curtains ... alongside the window-seat.

Then I rang one of the clip-joints.

I asked for Gunter and they, in turn, asked who was calling. I didn't tell them ... just that I wanted to talk with Gunter. Some mouthy bastard came on the phone, put what he thought were muscles into his voice and started talking like a back-street Humphrey Bogart.

I bit back.

I snarled, 'Hey—pansy-boy ... if you don't link me with Gunter *now*, he's liable to smear your lipstick next time he sees you.'

'Who the hell is that?' asked the mouthy man.

'Ask him,' I snapped.

'Uh?'

'Gunter ... if he thinks you should know, he'll tell you.'

In a much more flabby voice, the mouthy man said, 'He's not around ... that's jake. Gimme your number, and I'll tell him you called.'

'Find him,' I said.

'How the hell do I ...'

'You'll know,' I interrupted. 'If not you ... somebody. Find him. Fast! Tell him to contact me, urgently.'

'Who the hell ...'

'I like cricket,' I said, coldly. 'Tell him I like cricket ... and that he'd better be in touch. Unless he wants his wicket spread-eagled.'

I dropped the receiver onto its rest, before the mouthy man could work out any more questions.

He'd come ... I was as sure as tomorrow's sunrise.

The man with the mouth would contact him, because people like Gunter can *always* be contacted, and hicks like the mouthy comedian always know *where* to contact them. It runs parallel with the manager-secretary routine; the letter-taker in the front office always knows damn well where her boss is, but won't say, because not saying is part of what she is paid for. But, push things hard enough—and without saying much—and you'll reach him ... because, when the cows trot home, he needs you a damn sight more than you need him.

All I'd done was push.

Gunter was on the phone, within fifteen minutes.

He said, 'Ripley?'

I said, 'Let's not use names.'

'What's all this crap about cricket.'

'You will,' I said, softly, 'be carrying your bat back to the pavilion before much longer ... unless, of course, you wish for a prolonged innings.'

'Don't talk in riddles, friend.'

I snapped, 'And don't *you* talk stupid.'

There was a pause, then he said, 'Okay. Tell me where, when and how. That's all ...'

'Don't talk *stupid*,' I cut in.

There was another pause, then in a slightly less snappy voice, he said, 'Okay. Wrap it up in fancy talk. I'll understand.'

'Not over the telephone,' I said.

'Why the hell not? What the hell's wrong with ...'

'There are such things as tape-recorders,' I reminded him.

'Eh?'

'And they can be linked with telephones ... or didn't you know?'

'What the stink should I be doing taping a ...'

'Blackmail?' I suggested, innocently.

'Look—what is this, Ripley? What sort of a deal ...'

165

'I trust you, Gunter,' I said, sarcastically. 'I trust you as much as a tethered goat trusts a hungry tiger.'

'Look—we have a deal. I don't ...'

I rasped, 'Gunter, I'm out on a long, and not very safe, branch. And I'm not going to hand *you* the bloody saw. Do I make myself clear? There is such a game as Blackmail, and you are just the sort of bastard who might play that game. There are things you wanted to know. There are things I can tell you. Beyond that— nothing! ... not over telephone wires. This has to be an eyeball-to-eyeball thing, or I'm not interested. In the past, you've had a few quiet laughs at the way I walk. Play this thing any way, but *my* way, and you'll soon be envying me. Supposing they give you time off from the furnace to envy *anything*.'

I could hear the heavy breath come over the wire, before he said, 'Okay. I'll be out, tomorrow morning.'

'Don't bet money on it,' I snapped.

'As close as *that*. What the hell sort of ...'

Once more, I lowered the receiver to its resting place between the prongs.

It would get him ... too damn true it would get him. With a man like Gunter, guessing wasn't part of life; with him, any gambling was strictly after the winner had passed the post.

I knew crooks. Even crooks like Paul Gunter. *Especially* crooks like Paul Gunter. I had handled them—various types, various grades—too long not to know them. The bigger they were, the more suspicious ... and, in their world, 'suspicion' was another word for 'fear'.

I rolled the wheelchair to the window.

Outside, it was still light; that hard, sharp-edged light, which is the prelude to dusk.

I waited for the Peugeot.

About thirty minutes—less than three-quarters of an hour—later the Peugeot braked, outside the gate.

Gunter wasn't alone.

I should have expected it. I should have had the sense to know. I had subjected him to some very hard and urgent talk. Had I

166

been at the receiving end of that talk, and had I been Gunter, I might have suspected I was already breathing borrowed air. I would have taken basic precautions, pending having all the i's dotted and all the t's crossed.

It was what Gunter was doing.

Two heavies rode in the front of the Peugeot.

Gunter stayed in the rear, one heavy stayed at the wheel and kept the engine ticking over, and the second heavy opened the car door, closed it, made a quick, but careful, scrutiny of the landscape, strode up the path and made the big entrance ... and without knocking.

I heard the doors to each of the two bedrooms open, then close, in turn as the heavy worked his way from the hall. Then he moved into the living room, and I saw him for the first time.

He was tough ... and I do not mean make-believe-tough.

He had the broad-shouldered, slim-waisted, hard-eyed arrogance of the top-line tearaway. The genuine article. He opened the door with his left hand, and the fingers of his right hand stayed at chest-level ... obviously (so very obviously!) within easy snatching distance of a shoulder-holster.

He saw me, forgot me for a moment while he did a quick, visual tour of the room, then walked across and patted me about the waist and under the armpits. He had to bend to make the search, and his face came to within a few inches of mine. His breath smelled of peppermint.

'You have,' I commented, drily, 'seen too many gangster films. You should try Mickey Mouse, for a change ... it's just about your level.'

It was a little like talking to a brick.

He not only didn't answer, he obviously didn't even hear.

He did a fast walk round the room, then out and into the passage which leads from the hall. Into, and out of, the bathroom. Into the kitchen then—beyond the kitchen—I heard the rear door open. From outside, I heard the coal-house door open and close. Then the outside storehouse. Then the rear door closed and, a few seconds later the scout was back down the path, and at the gate, giving Gunter the signal to leave the Peugeot.

They came into the bungalow, and I heard the front door

close. Outside, in the Peugeot, I could see the second heavy with his hands resting on the wheel, moving his head slowly left and right, and ahead and towards the driving mirror ... suspicious, and ready to blast the horn at the slightest sign of trouble. I thought I could see a whisp of exhaust smoke coming from around the rear bumper; I was damn sure the engine was still ticking over ... ready for a possible getaway.

Gunter and his heavy walked into the living room.

The heavy closed the door, stood with his back to the wall, alongside the door—the hinge-side—so that, if the door opened he would, momentarily, be hidden. He slipped the gun from its shoulder-holster. A man-sized handgun. An automatic. Square and deadly; at a guess a Colt .45. He handled it as if the midwife hadn't been able to prize it from his fingers, at birth.

Everybody was hair-trigger edgy ... and that included me.

I said, 'The gun isn't necessary, Gunter. I'm on your side ... remember?'

'Nobody's on my side.' He glanced at the wheelchair. He growled, 'How come the baby-carraige?'

I said, 'When you don't have legs, you have to fall back on wheels ... sometimes.'

He grunted. As if one more minor point had been cleared up.

I played my first big bluff.

I said, 'All this fannying around. Haven't you heard of telescopic sights?'

'Meaning?'

'We are,' I said, 'going to switch a light on.'

'Who says?'

'This is still what is exaggeratedly known as my "castle", Gunter. You are—if anything—"guests". And I don't have cat's eyes.'

'Don't get fancy, Ripley,' he warned.

'Shit scared,' I sneered. 'Like all the rest of 'em. When the going looks like getting rough, you find the nearest rat-hole.'

'Ripley! I'm giving you the word. If you don't ...'

'Blow,' I snapped. 'Take off.'

'You could have a bullet right through that stupid face of yours.'

'I could,' I agreed. 'That way we'd all save money ... they could make it a double funeral.'

'As close as *that*?' In the gloom I saw his eyes narrow.

'You don't want to know,' I growled.

'We have a deal.'

'We *had* a deal ... use the right tense, Gunter.'

'What's with this, Ripley? What the hell ...'

'I do not,' I said, savagely, 'take kindly to gun-carrying goons hiking around my home, without my say-so. I do not take kindly to tin-plated big shots airing their muscles in my front room. I also like this carpet ... and I do not want it messed up with blood. Especially, I do not want it messed up with *your* blood.'

'They're out there,' he breathed, and his eyes sought the window and the gathering dusk, beyond.

I said, 'I wouldn't know. But, I wouldn't be surprised.'

I glanced at the heavy. His face was as expressionless as that of a corpse, but the colt was lined, perfectly, onto a point about three inches south of my tie-knot.

I tried to ignore the Colt, and said, 'I have limits, Gunter ... let's put it that way. "Options" ... that's what you call 'em. I need what you claim you can give me. But it has a price. I'll pay that price, but no more. There is no extra percentage for delivery. Part of my price is pride. What I have left of self-respect. I will talk to animals, like you. I will tell them what they want to know. But not with a gun pointing at me ... otherwise I might remember, and think I was scared. And not in half-light ... otherwise I might, again, remember and, this time, think I belonged in the same sewer. I want light. I want to see your face. I want to watch your eyes. I want Tom Mix, over there, to re-holster his six-shooter. And—on the off-chance—I do not want a killing in this house ... not even *you*. I'm the man who put you away, once ... remember? The only man ever to do it. That might make me a little bigger than most men you've met. I wouldn't know. I don't lay claim to it ... just that I *once* was. Either way, I like to think so. So-o, we draw the curtains. We switch on the lights. You tell your muscle-baby to stop waving his gun around. Otherwise ... you piss off. Now!'

Once upon a time—maybe when he was in his early teens—

somebody else must have used similar words to Paul Gunter. Somebody must have used a similar tone. But it was a long time ago ... and the odds were that, even *then*, he hadn't liked the experience.

This time, he liked it even less.

It was (I suppose) a little like Jehovah, being told by one of his Witnesses to go screw himself. It was (as far as Gunter was concerned) that much of a novelty.

Even the heavy looked mildly surprised ... and, with a man like that, mild surprise can be equated to any normal man's handstands and cartwheels.

I had them moving. I knew it. Like the mouse, seeing its first elephant—they didn't believe it ... except that it *was*.

Inside, I was one big grin. I'd pulled the first trick, and it was no David-Raff-and-soda-water-siphon gag, this time. Gunter was as near scared as such men can ever become; he was a little perplexed ... which, for him, was something he knew little about. I'd pulled it, because I was so low I'd have had to dig a hole to get any lower but, nevertheless, I'd snapped back at him and it had caught him off-balance. Like I say ... inside, I was one big grin.

Outside, I was nothing. I was all bluff. But I was *all* bluff ... I acted out the con with every tiny, movable muscle and every nuance of expression in my whole body. I hated Gunter with my eyes, and disdained him with the bend of my lips.

Coppers are actors. It goes with the job ... any copper worth his salary can give an Oscar-winning performance on the first cue of a crime-enquiry breakthrough. I'd had practice. I could do it and, this time, I did it well.

I left Gunter standing there, twisted the wheels of my chair and rolled to the window. Without waiting for anybody's say-so, I swished the curtains closed, and we were in darkness.

Gunter said, 'Switch on the light.' His voice was tight, but controlled and without a waver.

The room lights came on, and the heavy resumed his position against the wall, alongside the door. He still had the Colt in his fist, with a forefinger through the trigger-guard.

I said, 'Okay—now, be my guest, Gunter ... sit down.'

He took the seat I'd expected him to take. The one I'd willed him to take. The armchair positioned with its back at an angle to the window. I could see him but, without twisting his head, he couldn't see me.

The heavy did all the watching.

I said, 'Fine ... now the gun.'

'Look ...' began Gunter.

'The gun!' I snapped. 'If you need somebody to hold your hand, he can stay ...'

'He stays.'

'... but not with a gun in his hand.'

'Why not?'

'I may say something surprising. He may twitch his finger ... and once may be too many times.'

Gunter growled, 'He won't shoot, unless I say.'

'And I won't say, unless he shoves the shooter back into its case.'

'What the hell are you playing at Ripley?' snarled Gunter.

'Pride ...'

'Up my arse! What the hell ...'

'Take a walk, and die, Gunter,' I said, coldly. 'They have you on ice. You want to know how certain? I'll tell you ... call in at the undertakers, on the way back. Choose your own coffin.'

Part Two of the con coming up ... and it, also, worked.

The machinery creaked a little. The brake had almost seized. But Gunter forced himself—almost ruptured himself—but, eventually, made it.

He breathed, 'House the shooter.'

'Boss.' The heavy spoke for the first time. If you can imagine a face without expression looking worried, that was how the heavy looked. He began, 'I think you should ...'

'*House it!*' exploded Gunter.

And it was nice to hear the explosion. Gunter—the great Paul Gunter—was human, after all. Human enough to want to stay alive. Human enough to figure his own skin as being slightly more important than that of a certain detective constable (and the wife of that detective constable) of whom he hadn't given a damn.

The heavy nestled the Colt into its shoulder-holster, and I knew I had them ... right there, in the palm of my hand.

I had them!

All I had to do was close my fingers into a fist.

Gunter's face was back to deadpan, as he said, 'Okay, Ripley ... start earning yourself legs.'

'A neat way of putting it,' I murmured.

'Just talk. Just say something.'

'Certainly.' I rested my forearms on the arms of the wheelchair —with the fingers of my right hand within inches of the floor-length curtains—and said, 'Tomorrow—Sunday ... let's go through your normal routine.'

'I don't have a normal routine.'

'That's what you think,' I mocked. 'What you mean is that you do not run along rails. You don't have a stop-watch in your hand. That's what you mean. But you have a *routine*, Gunter. Broad, perhaps. Flexible, maybe. But it's there—a routine ... like everybody else on earth.'

'Look, what the hell are you ...'

'Go through it,' I suggested, teasingly. 'You—the man without a routine—go through it. You get out of bed ... right?'

He nodded. Tiny slow and suspicious nods of agreement.

'Same house. Same bedroom. Same bed. Right?'

'Right,' he grunted.

'And what next? Go to the bathroom? ... everybody goes to the bathroom. Maybe a shower—maybe a bath—maybe a shave ... the usual. Again, same room and, more or less, same time ... every day. A routine. Tomorrow. Sunday. Any damn day of the week, come to that. Then breakfast. Same room, same table, same chair ... same *everything*. You know the rest. I don't have to list everything. All the way through the day. Every day of your life ... except, maybe, holidays. That's *why* they're holidays. Because they temporarily break the pattern. But, most of the time, the pattern's there. It fluctuates, slightly—it alters a little, around the edges— but the general pattern stays constant ... every day. It *has* to, whoever you are. Everybody! It's known as "living" Gunter. And it makes you vulnerable. Even you.'

His voice wasn't quite as sure as he'd have liked it to have been, when he said, 'That's a crazy theory, Ripley. If that's all ...'

'Collins?' I said, softly.

'What about Collins?'

'You know him?'

'I know him,' he agreed.

'A very unusual copper.'

'He's ... dangerous,' he admitted, reluctantly.

'Make a note in your diary, Gunter,' I scoffed. 'You've just made the understatement of history.'

'All right ... he's *very* dangerous.'

I chuckled, quietly. As if at a subtle joke.

'This thing—whatever it is—is Collins's idea?' he asked harshly.

'Uhu ... all his own work.'

'The crazy man?'

'Raff?'

'Where does he come in?'

'Window dressing,' I murmured.

'It follows.' From the rear off-side, I saw his mouth twist into a sneer. 'So? It's Collins's scheme? Okay ... what is it?'

'We-ell, now ...' I moved my hands from the arms of the chair, and made a vague gesture. I dropped the right hand to behind the curtains, and the left hand onto the wheel of the chair, as I said, 'It goes something like this...'

The twelve-bore was exactly where it should have been; where I'd placed it, ready for this one-and-only chance. Hammers already cocked and the safety-catch to the 'Off' position.

I moved fast, but deliberately. My right hand gripped the shot-gun around the top of the stock, and just behind the breech. My index finger was curling the trigger, even as I slipped the gun from its hiding place.

I was also an expert with the chair—and why not? ... I'd had practice. Just the right amount of twist on the left wheel and, even as I tilted the shotgun into line across my chest and into the crook of my waiting left arm, its twin mouths were ready to spit

173

buckshot into the upper stomach of the heavy.

The heavy died. He died reaching for the shoulder-holster. He died in a lot of noise. He also died in a lot of blood ... and very suddenly.

His chest, and most of his guts, ended up as a very messy smear on the living room wall and door; a goodly percentage of him ended up as a mix with shattered plaster and chipped woodwork.

It is what happens when a man takes a twelve-bore cartridge at a range of less than twelve feet.

What also happens is noise.

Inside the confines of that room, the noise seemed to go on forever. Eardrum-bursting noise, which seemed to spin around the walls and bounce up and down, from floor to ceiling. Hell's own noise.

Which is why I screamed, '*UP!*'

And, fortunately for all concerned, Gunter heard me, and knew all the rules of this particular game. He stopped reaching for his pocket, and froze.

I touched his shoulder with the barrels of the shotgun, and he began to higher his hands.

I snapped, 'You have a gun, Gunter. Don't make a discussion out of it. Toss it into the middle of the room—*now* ... otherwise, I take you off by the neck.'

He nodded a single movement of complete understanding, dipped a hand into his jacket pocket, brought out a fancy, pearl-handled .32 revolver and threw it towards the far corner of the room.

Then, he clasped both hands on top of his head.

'Fine,' I breathed. 'You aren't a hero, after all.'

I moved. I knew I hadn't much time ... what I had could be counted in seconds.

I spun the wheels of the chair, with the shotgun within easy reach across the arms. I put the room's width between myself and Gunter, then dived a hand into my pocket, took out two fresh cartridges, broke the shotgun and had it re-loaded and re-cocked before the ejected empty and unused had had time to hit the carpet.

I grinned across at Gunter. I do not claim that it was a nice grin, or a friendly grin but, sure as hell, it was a contented grin.

I said, 'Just speak—that's all. Just move one hair of an eyebrow —that's all I ask ... *please*.'

He knew what I meant, and believed me.

We waited.

The other heavy (the one who'd passed his driving test) was expected. The reception committee was waiting to welcome him.

He'd come. After all that noise, he'd surely come. Plain or fancy—front or rear—door or window—he'd certainly come. All we had to do was wait.

We waited ... and he came.

He was a punk. He came in through the door, with as much finesse as a brush-salesman. He even shouldered the door when it jammed against the corpse of his fellow-soldier.

The last thing he heard, before he introduced himself to Old Nick, was Gunter's, 'You flaming bloody idiot!'

Which, as far as I was concerned, was a good enough epitaph.

I had a wrecked door, I had a ruined wall, I had some chipped and broken furniture, I had two shot-filleted hoodlums, the world could live without, I had a twin-barrelled shotgun, with one unused cartridge tucked neatly up the spout, I had Paul Gunter as a sitting, couldn't-miss-if-I-tried, target.

I had *everything*.

Gunter knew it. Gunter accepted it with a sardonic smile, and a glance of contempt at the body of the second heavy to end up with a cave where his guts should be.

'Why?' he asked, curiously.

'Guess,' I taunted.

He moved his shoulders, kept the fingers linked on top of his head, and said, 'I hand it to you, Ripley. Without legs, you're better than most men. *With* legs you could have been a world-beater.'

'With legs, this situation couldn't have happened,' I growled.

He moved his shoulders again, and said, 'Okay—I don't understand ... but what about the stiffs?'

'There'll be wreaths ... as always.'

He watched my face, and said, 'I can move them, Ripley.'

I looked puzzled—and for a reason ... I *was* puzzled.

I said, 'You know what's going to happen to you, Gunter? You do *know*?'

'Yeah.' He nodded. 'I still have options. One of them is a proposition.'

'More bribes?' I sneered.

'No.'

'More Swiss clinics?'

'There never was a Swiss clinic,' he admitted, amiably. 'That was a come-on ... which you maybe guessed.'

'Which I maybe guessed,' I grunted.

'Therefore, a straight proposition. No bribe. No come-on. Just something I want ... something only you can give me.'

I moved the barrels of the twelve-bore, and said, 'Put 'em down. On your lap. Just keep 'em in sight ... that's all.'

He unclasped his hands and dropped them onto his knees.

'Well?' I asked.

'You,' he said ... and, what the hell he meant (and, when he said it, I didn't know B from a bull's arse what he *did* mean) he was certainly serious.

'Draw pictures,' I suggested.

'You and me. We could ...' He moved his hands to emphasise something.

'Freeze!' I snapped.

He returned his hands to his knees.

He smiled, and said, 'That's what I mean, Ripley. What you've done—what you're capable of doing ... it makes you special.'

'What the hell *have* I done? I've killed two germs who didn't deserve to live. That's not clever, Gunter.'

'With a thousand other men,' he said softly, 'it would be more than clever ... it would be impossible. To murder ... just like that. It's not easy. To you, maybe. To you, sure ... you've proved it. But that doesn't make it easy. I control a lot of men, Ripley. Believe me. Some of them are rough. Some could do a muscle job, and enjoy the exercise. But not kill ... that's the dividing line. Accidentally ... okay. In a rough-house ... okay. But to point a gun, squeeze a trigger, and send a man over the edge, just because he's *there*. Not because you dislike him. Not because he's doing you dirt. Not because you even *know* him. Just to do it ... period. For a man like that I'd give a lot. For just one man, capable of pointing, squeezing and not even thinking ... he could write out his own cheque.'

In a soft, harsh voice, which I hardly recognised as my own, I said, 'And the option you mentioned?'

'The two of us.' He lifted his fingers, saw the tiny movement of the shotgun barrels, then lowered them without lifting his hands. He smiled, confidently, and said, 'We could tame the world, friend. Me, from where I am. You, from a wheelchair. We could tame the whole damn world. Together, we could ...'

'Where *you* are,' I interrupted, 'is at the wrong end of this twelve-bore. Where *I* am, all I need is a few ounces of pressure ... and you are *not*. The options are all used up, Gunter.'

His mouth lifted at one corner. The contempt was complete, and without even the hint of qualification.

The exchange was short-sentenced and packed hard with concentrated and mutual hatred.

'I'm not you,' he sneered.

'That, by ten, thank Christ!'

'I'm honest.'

'A cop-killer,' I rasped.

'A man-killer ... like you.'

'Those two? *Men?*'

'I've said ... I'm honest.'

'You are bloody unique,' I snarled.

'No ... two of us.'

'Not like you ... not in a million years.'

'Con yourself, Ripley. Don't con *me*.'

In a near-scream, I yelled, 'It's coming, Gunter. Watch the birdie!'

I put sudden pressure on the trigger and, for the third time, noise ripped through the room; noise almost loud enough to be solid; noise which seemed to roar on far too long; noise which deafened me, blinded me and, for a time, tore my senses away from my body.

And Gunter was dead.

And somebody, somewhere, was going to have the job of

burying a headless corpse; I'd done what I'd threatened to do ...
I'd taken him off at the neck.

It took me a long time to fix up the cassette-player and the
microphone. From a wheelchair, I had to shift two hunks of
stiffening flesh, before I could jerk the smashed door wide enough
to give me passage. Then, I had to manoeuvre around the
carnage to do all the plugging in and positioning of the
microphone.

It took me a long time ... almost an hour.

Then I slipped the last cassette into the slot, and I was ready.

Ah, yes ... but ready for *what*?

Ready to say I've rid the world of Paul Gunter? Ready to
make it known that Detective Constable Fixby, and his wife,
Paulette Fixby, have been avenged? That they may now rest in
peace? That nobody *can* kill a cop—not even Paul Gunter—and
get away with it?

Could be.

Could be that is what I want to say ... but if it is, it is only
part of it, and some people might only say a small part.

For the last few seconds of his life, I hated Gunter. I truly
hated him, with a depth and with a senseless, groping passion
I never thought possible. I squeezed that trigger with black joy
burning bright inside me, and the only regret was that the killing
had, of necessity, to be both swift and (for all I know) painless.
My choice, at that moment, would have made it agonising, and
would have made the agony last until the final second of
eternity.

That was the size of my hatred.

But next question—*why*?

Not merely because he'd killed a policeman. Policemen die—
policemen are killed—and, although the rest of the force mourns
and (if the killing is deliberate) hounds the killer, there is anger

178

but no true hatred ... not the hell's own hatred I felt for Gunter. Not that brand of hatred. Fixby had been a copper ... but I hadn't known him. I'd met his wife once—that's all ... and might not have known her for who she was, had not Gunter walked into *The Woodchopper's Arms.*

So, who am I kidding? That I killed Gunter, and two of his minders, as retribution for the death of Fixby and his wife? Just who the hell am I *kidding?*

Which, in turn, begs the question of the hatred.

I killed the two heavies because, had they lived, I might not have been able to kill Gunter ... okay, that answers the questions raised by two corpses.

I enticed Gunter to the bungalow, in order that I might kill *him* ... and that answers the questions of the third, and most important, corpse.

But why all that hatred?

Damn it, at first—when Collins and Raff first approached me, in *The Silver Bowl*—I didn't even want to kill him. I wanted no part of it. All along, I've counted it a crazy idea. Stupid. Impossible. Something to be dreamed up by loons, but dismissed by men of even average mentality. All along, that has been my belief.

Yes ... even when Gunter promised to make me walk again. Even when I believed him; when I allowed wishful thinking to smother common gumption; when I played ducks and drakes with loyalty and friendship.

Even then!

One pea-sized corner of my mind knew (knew damn well!) that I was lying in my own teeth. Had there been a hope—*any* hope— Elaine would have rooted it out, and would have made me turn that hope into a certainty.

So-o ...

I knew what I was doing, and I knew I was being conned.

But, even then, I didn't hate Gunter ... did I hell as hate him! Time was, when I almost admired him. When I made silent excuses for him; excuses for his excess of evil; excuses for every crime he'd ever committed or was ever likely to commit. In effect, I called him a giant (which he certainly was) but ignored the fact that a giant is large in all things ... and, sometimes, one of those things is villainy.

I admired him, because he didn't scare.

Even at the end he wasn't scared ... and, when the end came, I *didn't* admire him.

He wasn't scared, because ... We-ell, now—could be, because he was brave. Could be, because his philosophy was so complete that he accepted the inevitable ... that, in time, all men die. Could be, that he was a little tired of life ... although I doubt that. Could be, that he was so damn sure I wouldn't blast him with the twelve-bore. Could be, that he lacked the necessary imagination which fear demands; a lettuce isn't frightened when it's shredded for a salad ... and some people have the imaginative intelligence of a lettuce. Could be, that Gunter was that sort of man ... with the imaginative intelligence of a lettuce.

Could also be, that I'm still kidding myself.

The offer he made ... it might have been genuine. It was the sort of offer he could so easily have made. And meant it. A 'trigger man' ... that was the job he was offering. The genuine paid killer; the man who kills, not merely without mercy, but also without passion. Without feeling. With neither the joy of the pathologically twisted, nor even the feeling of distasteful necessity felt (presumably) by a public hangman. Without emotion of any kind, or any degree. He kills, because he is a 'killer'; because it is his profession, and as simple a profession (or, if you like, as complicated a profession) as that of a plumber. Or a house-painter. Or a crane-driver.

He is a tradesman—an artisan—and that his 'trade' happens to be murder in no way shocks him, or causes him concern.

The true *killer* ... could be, that Gunter figured me as one such unique being.

He was wrong.

Or, *was* he?

I butchered three men in the course of fifteen minutes ... less.

As far as the first two were concerned, they were in the way and I 'removed' them. Just that. No hesitation. No repugnance. No feeling of guilt, or disgust. They were criminals—okay ... but they were also men. I didn't even know them. Maybe they had wives. Maybe they had families. Maybe they were both good husbands and loving fathers ... and many criminals are, at least, *that*. I slaughtered them, without feeling and for no better reason than that they were in a certain place at a certain time. They were in the way. They were 'inconvenient'. Therefore they died.

For Christ's sake! ... was Gunter *right*?

Am I really such a bastard, and did Gunter recognise me for what I am?

Is that why I hated him so absolutely, at the end?

Am I what *he* was? ... and probably worse?

If so, it explains the hatred. It explains such a lot of things.

Tell Susan I love her—loved her ... still love her. She'll know ... but remind her, anyway.

Don't let her hear these tapes. Tell her ...

No! Don't tell her anything. She'll understand, without being told.

I, too, understand. Talking it out, like this—then listening to it being played back—has solved some of the problems. The 'starting place', for example. I had, if you remember, some difficulty in pinpointing the 'starting place' of this sequence of events, when I began.

Now, I know.

It wasn't that day when I first met Gunter; that interview room in Beechwood Brook nick. It wasn't then. It wasn't when the bullet nicked my spine, either. Nor was it at Collins's retirement party, at *The Woodchopper's Arms* ... it was well under way, by that time.

It started with a death; with a heart attack, and the complete tilting of my whole world. That's when it started ... and that's why this *had* to happen.

Don't mourn. Don't weep. If certain people are to be believed (and who am I to doubt them?) my world has, by this time, straightened itself out again.

I am, once more, happy.

*   *   *

The stereo speakers cut into the Berlioz Symphonie Fantastique. *It happened with instantaneous abruptness; as if the word 'happy' had carried a magical quality, and had flung open great doors to let loose a flood of sound.*

Collins walked to the hi-fi set-up, touched a switch, and the music was guillotined into silence.

Sullivan watched him, from the comfort of one of the ox-blood-leather wing-chairs.

'From the grave,' murmured Sullivan.

Collins slipped the cassette from its slots and added it to the neat stack of cassettes on the military-chest coffee-table.

He said, 'Drinks, I think.'

He went to the settle—to where an oval, silver tray containing glasses and a decanter, was already waiting on the green baize of the seat—and carried the tray to the military-chest coffee-table. He poured drinks; good sherry, in attractive, man-sized glasses. He handed a glass to Sullivan, then seated himself in the other wing-chair.

He said, 'Shall we drink a toast, Richard? To a brave man?'

Sullivan moistened his lips, from the glass.

Collins sipped at his sherry, and said, 'To an uncommonly honest man.'

'And a man,' said Sullivan, slowly, 'who has left some uncommonly odd questions unanswered.'

'Really?' There was gentle surprise in the question.

Sullivan placed his glass on the tray. He crossed his legs, then linked fingers across the front of his bent knee. When he spoke, it was in a tone part-questioning and part-musing.

He said, 'All right. He blew his own foot off. A hell of a way to commit suicide. A slow way ... to allow yourself to bleed to death. I—er—I didn't know about the gangrene. He told me it was a twisted ankle, and I believed him. But—y'know ... a hell of a way to commit suicide.'

'Painless,' said Collins, quietly. 'A little like going to sleep ... getting drowsy, then dying.'

'I wouldn't know,' grunted Sullivan.

'The élite of the Roman Empire chose a similar way,' said Collins. 'In a bath—blood-heat ... they merely opened a vein.

Then—er—they dropped off. No pain. No cramp. Nothing. The only truly comfortable mode of self-destruction ... that's what the experts say.'

'I wouldn't know.'

Collins said, 'Gibbon mentions it. It's also referred to in Ben Hur, and Quo Vadis. In many ways, the Romans had a superb civilisation.'

'Suicide ... with all mod cons,' growled Sullivan.

Collins smiled, gently.

'He read a lot.'

'Quite a lot,' agreed Collins.

'More than usual.'

'No-o ... I wouldn't say that, Richard. No more than I read.'

'You're not "usual". And—er—you chose a lot of his books. Right?'

'I introduced him to certain authors, if that's what you mean.'

'I don't know what the hell I mean,' said Sullivan, irritably. 'That's the trouble ... I don't know what I do mean. But the foot—blowing his own foot off, and letting himself bleed to death. That's still a cockeyed way of committing suicide. In my opinion.'

'Forget the ... what you call "all mod cons".' Collins tasted his drink. 'The foot was symbolic. It was dead ... what he wished himself to be. It was rotten ... as corrupt as, at one point, he himself was tempted to become. And—remember, he loved his daughter—by doing it that way, he saved Susan the horror of looking at a mangled corpse. The shroud covered the stump. It was sad ... but not horrific.'

'An answer for everything,' muttered Sullivan, trenchantly.

'There usually is,' agreed Collins.

'He put the tapes—these cassette things—away. In the safe. Gave you the combination. Why you? Why, specifically you?'

'It had to be somebody.'

'Yes ... but why you?'

'Somebody he could trust.'

'And he could trust you?'

'It would seem so.'

Sullivan paused, frowned then, very softly, said, 'Why?'

'My dear Richard, I've already ...'

'No! I mean why did he kill him? Why kill Gunter? Why kill the other two? Why kill himself? God almighty ... why do it all, in the first place?'

'Richard.' Collins smiled, and the smile was gentle, but filled with compassionate wisdom. It was a sad smile, but a smile which held other things than sadness. An understanding of human weaknesses. A slight chiding at some of the stupidities and weaknesses of the human race. The smile—and the speaking of the christian name of the man to whom he spoke—held all these qualities ... and more. He sipped at the wine, then said, 'One year, nine months and four days. Charles knew to the day. He claimed to know to the minute—almost to the second ... and I believe him. He waited for death, all that time. Longed for it. I knew him —you knew him ... we both know that he was incomplete. That, even had he had the full use of all his limbs, he would still have been incomplete. His feelings—his true feelings—reflected themselves in his choice of music. In the sort of books he enjoyed. In what he knew about art, and the sort of art which sparked off his imagination. Even in the choice of where he lived ... alone, and cut off from the rest of the world, as if he was already entombed.

'He was inordinately proud of his masculinity. A "man's man" ... that's the term he'd have used, to describe himself. A policeman, and a good policeman. Which, by his yardstick, meant he was tough. Hard. Ruthless. That's how he thought of himself, and what he believed himself to be. But he was wrong. Hopelessly wrong. Idiotically wrong.

'Charles Ripley was a romantic ... in the broadest, and finest, sense of that word. He fell in love once, in all his life. With his wife, Elaine. She left him for a time ... he played the role of tough policeman too well, and she couldn't tolerate it. She left him. But, when she came back, he was waiting for her. Eager for her. Happy that she was able to forgive him, and accept him for what he was. He didn't try to find another woman. As far as he was concerned, it was Elaine ... or nobody. He was a romantic.

'Proof of it? He was a Manic Depressive ... he said so. He described it well. You know what that means, Richard?'

184

'Tell me,' grunted Sullivan. 'You're doing all the talking.'

Collins repeated his slow, wise smile, and said, 'Peaks and valleys. That's what it boils down to. An elation—joy—happiness unknown to non-sufferers. Then troughs of depression. Misery—suicidal misery ... and without apparent cause. Manic Depression ... it's the disease of the romantics, Richard. It's what makes the romantics of art—any art-form—different from all other artists. Bach wasn't ... Tchaikovsky was. Van Gogh was, so was Toulouse-Lautrec ... but not Leonardo da Vinci. It doesn't make for greatness. Not in itself. It isn't even necessary for greatness. But it makes a difference. Always! It's recognisable. Especially by fellow Manic Depressives. It touches something. They don't know what ... just that it always does. An understanding, if you like. What the feelings were of the man who painted this particular picture, or composed this particular piece of music. It's always there ... always!'

Sullivan unclasped his fingers, reached for his glass and swallowed a mouthful of sherry. He replaced the glass, re-linked his hands in front of his crossed knee, and frowned.

He said, 'What you're trying to explain is ...'

He closed his mouth, and deepened his frown.

'That Charles was never what he pretended to be,' said Collins.

'Are any of us?'

'No-o,' agreed Collins, slowly.

'So?'

'At the end ...' Collins placed his glass alongside Sullivan's, on the tray, unfolded himself from the wing-chair, walked to one of the walls of the room and, as he talked, stared at the two Dürers. He said, 'At the end, he knew what it was all about. He knew everything—had guessed everything ... he as much as said so. He likened the game to chess.'

'The game?'

'The killing of Paul Gunter.' Collins raised a hand and flicked a dust mote from the glass behind which was the Study of Plants. He explained it ... but Gunter didn't understand.'

'Y'mean ...'

'You know exactly what I mean, Richard,' Collin's voice carried the hint of weary impatience.

Sullivan said, 'He described Raff as "window dressing".'

'Quite.'

'But—but ...' Sullivan floundered a little. 'That means ...'

'It means ...' Collins turned to face Sullivan. His voice was cold and irritable, and his expression matched his tone. He shoved his hands into his trouser pockets, and said, 'It means Paul Gunter is dead ... which is what I promised. He was a criminal, who deserved to die. He killed a police officer, therefore he deserved to die. He offended my guests, the other evening at The Woodchopper's Arms—he offended one of them so badly that she took her own life—therefore he deserved to die. That, if you like, was the "motive".

'I needed David Raff because, as far as Gunter was concerned, David was capable of anything. Anything! Therefore, with David, it was even possible to envisage a trio of ex-senior police officers planning murder ... the murder of Paul Gunter, that is.

'I needed Charles as somebody Gunter would approach. Somebody not of this force. I knew he wouldn't try Raff. He would never be foolish enough to try me. Therefore, Charles Ripley ... the obvious choice.

'The obvious choice for another reason, too. The obvious, and the only, choice. Ripley, himself. One year, nine months and four days ago, he'd have committed suicide. Listen to the tapes, Richard. Remember the man we both knew as Charles Ripley. He would have committed suicide then! He wanted to. All—except one thing—urged him to take his own life, and join the only woman he'd ever loved in eternity. He wasn't quite the "Romeo" to her "Juliet" ... that's all. His infernal masculinity stood in the way. He was "tough". He could "take it". He was a romantic—he was a Manic Depressive—and, as sure as God made green apples, every fibre screamed for him to join her ... but he couldn't. Because of what he'd made himself believe. About himself. Men—"he-men"—don't die for love. Not that way. Not self-destruction, because they can't live without one woman. That would be "weak" ... in their eyes. A weakness. Something of which to be ashamed.

'I gave him something of which to be proud. I gave him Paul Gunter—gave him the pleasure of killing the most obnoxious

186

person I've ever met ... and a good enough reason for taking his own life. A "man's" reason.'

'You "gave" him Gunter You mean you ...'

'All right, Richard. All right.' Collins gave a tired twist of the lips as his shoulders drooped. He looked weary; bone weary, and he walked across to the chair he'd vacated, flopped into it and rested his neck against its back. He closed his eyes, and said, 'Chapter and verse, Richard. That's what you want. That's what you can have. The cassettes ... they're useless. The "automatic wipe" switch was down while they were playing. They're clean. Charles's voice isn't on them any more. But I thought you should hear his story—his side of it, if you like—before I destroyed it.

'Charles guessed ... before he died. That, basically, it was I who killed Paul Gunter. That I merely used Charles as a means to an end. A tool. A weapon ... as much of a weapon as the shotgun Charles himself used.

'The restaurant—The Silver Bowl—it was one of Gunter's main listening-posts in the city. He controlled it—owned it, in fact ... I've known that for years.'

'The hell you have!' breathed Sullivan.

'Motive. Means. Opportunity. They inter-linked, beautifully.' Collins opened his eyes, turned his head and smiled, sadly, at Sullivan. 'The perfect murder, Richard. I'm sorry ... it must be very hard on your ego. I warned you I would. And I have. And— face it my friend—there isn't a damn thing you can do about it.'